About the Book

When Mr. Squeers, the Square Toe City photographer, tells Miss Pickerell that her face has too many fatigue lines in it, she knows it is time for her to take a rest. She leaves for a vacation at the Three Chimney Lodge by the very next train.

But peace and quiet are not what she finds there. On the day following her arrival, she is already down in the oily depths of a supertanker, trying to repair a leak. Nothing can stop her when she realizes that the oil spill is killing sea birds and water creatures all around.

She defies the threats of the menacing Mr. Lovelace, the lodge proprietor. She risks drowning when the air hose connected to her aqua lung rips open. And with the help of her new young friend, Mortimor Tooting, she dares to breed the oil-eating supermicrobes that even the scientists have not risked testing outside the laboratory.

In this, her twelfth adventure, Miss Pickerell breathes her famous "Forevermore" many times. It gives her the courage to complete her mission of love.

MISS PICKERELL
and the
SUPERTANKER

MISS PICKERELL
and the
SUPERTANKER

by Ellen MacGregor and Dora Pantell

Illustrated by Charles Geer

McGRAW-HILL BOOK COMPANY

New York • St. Louis • San Francisco • Auckland
Düsseldorf • Johannesburg • Bogotá • London
Madrid • Mexico • Montreal • New Delhi • Panama • Paris
São Paulo • Singapore • Sydney • Tokyo • Toronto

IN MEMORY OF FIGIE, THE WISE AND BEAUTIFUL CAT

WHO WAS MY FRIEND FOR SIXTEEN YEARS,

AND

FOR JENNIFER, THE LITTLE GIRL I ADORE

MISS PICKERELL AND THE SUPERTANKER

Copyright © 1978 by McGraw-Hill, Inc. All Rights Reserved. Printed in
the United States of America. No part of this publication may be
reproduced, stored in a retrieval system, or transmitted, in any form or by
any means, electronic, mechanical, photocopying, recording, or otherwise,
without the prior written permission of the publisher.

Library of Congress Cataloging in Publication Data

MacGregor, Ellen.
    Miss Pickerell and the supertanker.

    SUMMARY: Miss Pickerell sets out to have a restful vacation but finds
herself involved in the problem of a leaky supertanker and its pollution of
the sea.
    [1. Oil pollution of rivers, harbors, etc.—Fiction] I. Pantell, Dora, joint
author. II. Geer, Charles. III. Title.
PZ7.M1698Mhc   [Fic]   7 8-8241
ISBN 0-07-044588-5

Contents

1

THE SUPERTANKER AT THE SURPRISE PARTY

Miss Pickerell looked out at the scene of her surprise Valentine's Day party with increasing dismay. From where she stood at the top of the steps outside her kitchen door, she could see her seven nieces and nephews and all the other junior members of THE MISS PICKERELL FAN CLUB, SQUARE TOE MOUNTAIN BRANCH, inside the house and out. It was only a little after 10:00 in the morning but they were already stuffing themselves with extra thick slices of chocolate cake covered with two layers of heavy whipped cream. She shuddered slightly, tucked a loose hairpin into place, and turned her attention to the senior members of the club. They were mostly carrying tables, chairs, and trays full of paper cups and peppermintade from the kitchen out to the vegetable garden in back of the farmhouse. The day was unusually warm and although patches of snow still lay on the ground, Mrs. Broadribb, Senior Vice-President of THE MISS PICKERELL FAN CLUB, SQUARE TOE MOUNTAIN BRANCH, had decided to move the entire party outdoors. Miss Pickerell moved down the steps to be out of the way and pressed herself against the wall under the kitchen window.

"I suppose," she commented to Pumpkins, her big black cat who was sitting high up on the windowsill where he could feel *almost* sure that no one would reach him, "I suppose it would be easier if I knew who all these children and their mothers and fathers were. They seem to have come from the whole county."

Pumpkins thumped his tail to show he was listening.

"And I'm certain," Miss Pickerell added thoughtfully, "that it would be much more polite if I didn't just stand here. After all, they've gone to such a lot of trouble to make this party for me. I'll go and say *something* to them."

She pushed her glasses more securely up on her nose and looked around for a good place to start. Mr. Esticott, Square Toe City's chief train conductor, stood a few feet to her left, talking to her friend Mr. Kettelson, the hardware store man. Miss Pickerell observed that Mr. Esticott had lost some weight, mainly over the stomach where the silver buttons of his uniform never used to meet the buttonholes. But his jacket now hung lower in the front than in the back and he seemed even more nervous than usual. Mr. Kettelson, who was always sad, had a particularly mournful expression on his face and a deep frown between his bushy eyebrows.

"I'd better not start with them," Miss Pickerell decided. "Not if I don't want to hear how bad the hardware store business is doing from Mr. Kettelson. And Mr. Esticott is sure to tell me about some disaster he has heard of somewhere."

She turned to her right, where Miss Lemmon, the local telephone operator and recording secretary of THE MISS PICKERELL FAN CLUB, SQUARE TOE MOUNTAIN BRANCH, sat on a camp stool, a large pad of yellow paper in her lap. She had taken off her hat and was busy puffing out the sleeves of her pink party dress. Mrs. Broadribb stared disapprovingly at the matching ribbon in Miss Lemmon's thinning gray hair when she passed with a platter of heart-shaped sugar buns. Mrs. Broadribb was wearing faded blue jeans and a baggy sweatshirt and her ample bosom heaved when she put the heavy platter down on a table and let out a sigh.

Miss Pickerell sighed too. The children were becoming noisier and noisier. Most of them—her oldest niece, Rosemary, and her middle nephew, Euphus, among them—were milling about at the far end of the garden, near the oak tree where the locusts sang in the summer. Unlike the locusts, the children seemed to be able to chew with their mouths open and to keep chattering at the same time. Miss Pickerell took a deep breath and moved resolutely toward them. They surrounded her instantly, jumping up and down and talking all at once.

"We want to see Nancy Agatha, your cow," a small girl with two pigtails squealed. "Euphus said we could."

"Euphus said so! Euphus said so!" two boys standing behind her shouted.

"We heard him! We heard him!" three boys and a girl, pushing to get up in front, called out.

"Euphus did! Euphus did! Euphus did!" everybody else screamed.

Miss Pickerell put her hands over her ears and peered forward to give Euphus a hard stare. Why, she would no more dream of disturbing her beloved cow with a bunch of screeching . . . The piping voice of the child with the pigtails turned her thoughts away from Euphus for the moment.

"I have a cow, too," the little girl said. "And a puppy dog with long ears."

"I have three cats and two guinea pigs," an unusually tall boy added.

"I have a hamster and a lot of fish," another boy boasted. "I sent you a picture of them in my letter."

"I want a picture of *you*, Miss Pickerell," the tall boy said.

"A picture of you! A picture of you!" every child begged.

"Order! Order! Everybody, order!" a voice boomed suddenly from under the kitchen window, where Mr. Rugby, the stout Senior President of THE MISS PICKERELL FAN CLUB, SQUARE TOE MOUNTAIN BRANCH and owner of the Square Toe County Diner, stood unsteadily on a wobbly folding chair. He wore a tall, freshly starched chef's hat on his head and held a whistle in his hand. His double chins bounced as he looked across the garden at Miss Pickerell.

"In my position as Senior President," he announced, "I am ready to start the program. The opening number is a drama prepared by the children in THE MISS PICKERELL FAN CLUB, PLENTIBUSH CITY BRANCH."

The drama turned out to be a playlet in which Mr. Esticott's youngest granddaughter, who lived in Plentibush City, was the star and kept reciting, "Miss Pickerell can do anything, and to her, our love we bring." Everybody applauded and ate the caramel custard that Rosemary was passing around, while they listened to Mr. Rugby who was now making a speech.

"Miss Pickerell is the bravest lady in the world," he said. "Absolutely the . . ."

"Oh, pooh!" Miss Pickerell declared.

"She has been down in the ocean and up in outer space," Mr. Rugby went on. "She has traveled to Mars and to the moon. She has braved the fury of the monster robot, Mr. H.U.M., and the cunning of that deadly kidnapper who called himself Mr. H.H.

Harding. She has even defied the perils of earthquakes and floods. Who knows where her courageous spirit will lead her next? Who . . . ?"

Miss Pickerell stopped listening.

"Never again," she muttered between tightly clenched teeth. "I never had any intention of getting mixed up in those dangerous escapades. And I'm *certainly* not going to now!"

She trembled violently from head to toe at the very idea and quickly glanced around to make sure nobody had noticed. Most of the faces were turned to Mr. Rugby, who seemed to be finishing his speech. Rosemary, sitting under the oak tree with Euphus, was the first to applaud. Euphus kept on writing something on a piece of paper. Miss Pickerell didn't blame him for not paying close attention to the speech. She thought he should *look* as though he were listening, however. She was just making a mental note to discuss this with Euphus when Mr. Rugby blew his whistle and announced the next number on the program.

"A toast to Miss Pickerell," he said. "Composed by her young fans. It will be sung by the chorus, which I will lead."

The chorus lined up on the kitchen steps. Miss Pickerell recognized two of the boys. Their voices hadn't changed yet and they sang soprano. Her friend, Professor Humwhistel, who worked in the space laboratory right outside of Square Toe City, sang the tenor solo. He looked very dignified with his beard neatly brushed and his gold-rimmed spectacles dangling from a wide velvet ribbon attached to his vest. One of his shoelaces was loose, though, and dragging on the ground. Miss Pickerell was not surprised. Professor Humwhistel was extremely absentminded. He didn't even notice the shoelace as he stood on the top step, signaling for everybody to drink their peppermintade and to join him in the verse!

"We love your cat and cow, Miss Pickerell
We love Pumpkins' loud meow
We love your heart so bold, Miss Pickerell
We love you, young and old."

And then the party began to break up. Parents called out to children that it was time to go home. Mrs. Broadribb and Miss Lemmon started to clear the tables. Mr. Esticott and Mr. Kettelson carried folded

tables and chairs back into the house. Rosemary went along to show them where to put
everything. Miss Pickerell, grateful for the
sudden quiet, went to sit down on her
kitchen steps. Mr. Rugby, Euphus, and Professor Humwhistel sat down with her.

"I have a list for you, Miss Pickerell," Mr.
Rugby said, handing her a crumpled piece

of paper. "Euphus was good enough to write down the names and addresses of everybody who was here."

"So that you can send them the pictures they want," Euphus explained.

Miss Pickerell carefully examined the list. It extended to the bottom of the page and over onto the back. Here, the names and addresses were scribbled in between other words. Miss Pickerell read some of them out loud, though she was not completely sure that she was pronouncing them all correctly.

"Hydrocarbons!" she said slowly. "Plasmids! Oil-eating microbes! Simultaneous versus individual components and their breakdown . . . Euphus, what is all this?"

"Oh, nothing," Euphus muttered. "I was just trying to do some of my science homework while Mr. Rugby was talking."

"I noticed that," Miss Pickerell commented.

"I believe," Professor Humwhistel explained, "that Euphus is talking about oil spills. Or oil slicks, as they are more professionally referred to."

Miss Pickerell beamed at Euphus. She really felt very proud of her middle nephew. Most boys of his age did not know half as much about science as he did. Professor Humwhistel often told her that this was his opinion, too.

"Oil spills from tankers," Euphus was explaining to her now. "The spills from a medium-sized tanker can leave about 200,000 gallons of oil in the water and it can spread for miles around."

"I saw in the newspaper," Mr. Rugby said, "that a supertanker ran aground a week ago. A customer showed me the story. It was on the last page. I don't always get to the last page when I read the daily paper."

"Did you say *supertanker*?" Miss Pickerell asked, getting back to the point. "A supertanker?"

"A supertanker," Professor Humwhistel said, nodding, "The one Mr. Rugby is talking about was a gigantic 824 feet long, the size of two whales, nose to tail. It had five main oil storage tanks that descended 100 feet. When it ran aground on a shoal, its steel hull was punctured, I'm afraid."

"Forevermore!" breathed Miss Pickerell.

"And the oil that it spilled," Mr. Rugby added, "killed everything within minutes."

"No!" Miss Pickerell gasped.

"It did too," Euphus insisted. "Fish, sea birds, ocean plant life, everything!"

"Crude oil brings on a terrible death," Professor Humwhistel said quietly. "It poisons and suffocates the life that it reaches."

Miss Pickerell could hardly believe her ears. She stared furiously at Euphus and at Mr. Rugby and at Professor Humwhistel.

"Why doesn't somebody stop those oil spills?" she demanded, her blood practically boiling with indignation. "I will go call the Governor! Immediately!"

Professor Humwhistel put out his hand to stop her as she stood up and began to climb the kitchen steps.

"I'm afraid . . . I'm afraid . . ." he began.

"Yes?" Miss Pickerell asked. "Please go on, Professor Humwhistel."

"Well," Professor Humwhistel said slowly, "the causes of oil spills are not always the same."

"A hurricane can cause a spill," Mr. Rugby offered. "Or a blizzard. Or a collision."

"Or a bad ship design," Professor Humwhistel added. "Or faulty navigational equipment. Higher standards would do much to help keep the oil inside the tankers where—"

"I think," Euphus interrupted, "that the tankers are too big."

"Yes," Professor Humwhistel agreed, nodding vigorously. "There would certainly be much less damage from oil spilled out of smaller tankers."

"You can call the Governor about *that*!" said Euphus, happily. "Tell him, 'No More Supertankers!'"

"I don't believe," Professor Humwhistel said, standing up and sighing, "that the Governor can accomplish this change overnight. But . . ."

"Yes?" Miss Pickerell asked, prompting him again.

"But," Professor Humwhistel went on, "I believe that there is reason for great hope in a different direction. Scientists are now working on a method of preventing the disasters that the oil spills bring about."

"With oil-eating microbes!" Euphus shouted.

"Yes," Professor Humwhistel agreed quietly. "But unfortunately, it is a slow process. The development of a method that will prove to be truly successful may still take months, perhaps years. Who knows?"

He sighed heavily as he took his unlit pipe out of one of his jacket pockets. Then he began searching for his matches in another.

"That same customer I was telling you about," Mr. Rugby said, "he told me that there was another oil spill only last week. And one the week before. That one killed almost *everything* in that area."

"Not too far from here, I believe," Professor Humwhistel, now searching in the pockets of his vest, commented absently.

"Oh, very far," Mr. Rugby said. "My customer told me that he . . ."

Miss Pickerell left them to go on with their argument and walked up the steps to her kitchen. She felt suddenly very tired. Mrs. Broadribb, putting the last of the paper cups into the garbage bin, looked up at her.

"You seem a little pale, Miss Pickerell," she said. "Aren't you feeling well?"

"Not very," Miss Pickerell admitted. "I think I'll go upstairs and lie down for a while."

"You needn't worry about your cow," Mr. Kettelson assured her, as he placed a washed pitcher that Miss Lemmon handed him up on a top shelf. "I just ran out to the upper pasture to see her. She's fine."

"Thank you, Mr. Kettelson," Miss Pickerell smiled.

"It's those children," Miss Lemmon suggested. "Their screeching can make anyone sick."

"It wasn't the children," Miss Pickerell replied.

"Oh?" Miss Lemmon, Mrs. Broadribb, and Mr. Kettelson asked.

"It . . . it was that supertanker," Miss Pickerell said, speaking half to herself.

"What supertanker?" Mr. Kettelson inquired. "What supertanker, Miss Pickerell?"

"The supertanker at the surprise party," Miss Pickerell answered grimly as, followed by Pumpkins, she walked toward the curving wooden staircase that led up to her bedroom.

2

DOWN THE MOUNTAIN ON A MODEL-T BIKE

Halfway up the stairs, Miss Pickerell remembered that she could never sleep during the day.

"And there's no use in my trying," she murmured as she walked into her bedroom and sat down in her corner rocking chair. "But I have to be alone for a while. I have to *think*."

She thought again of calling the Governor. Of course, Professor Humwhistel had practically said that the Governor couldn't help, and she had to agree. Science was not at all his line of work.

"Anyway," she commented to Pumpkins, who was busy making himself comfortable on the crocheted quilt that was spread across the foot of the shining brass bed, "anyway it's Saturday. I don't really want to disturb him on his day off."

She got up out of the rocker and began walking around the room.

"The only thing I *can* do," she told herself, "is to try to get my mind *off* those oil tankers. Maybe I should rearrange the bureau drawers."

She started with the handkerchief drawer on the top right-hand side. It didn't seem to need any reorganizing. The plain white handkerchiefs lay in one neat pile, the flowered ones in another, and those with the lace edging all around them in a third. Some of the handkerchiefs looked a little creased, though. Miss Pickerell took them out and put them aside for ironing.

"Better still, I'll wash them," she said. "They can use some freshening up."

The drawer next to the handkerchiefs held her balls of wool, her knitting needles, and her crochet hooks. The wools were arranged by color, the light ones in front and the dark ones in the back. The knitting needles and the crochet hooks all had pieces of tape pasted on them and their numbers were clearly printed with black laundry ink on each tape. There was nothing, Miss Pickerell saw, that she could do to make this drawer look any better. There was nothing she needed to do with the rest of the bureau drawers, either.

"Oh, dear!" she sighed.

She sat down again in the rocking chair, leaned way back, and stared up at the ceiling. It had a strip of ornamental molding like a little shelf running all around. Rosemary often advised her that the molding was very old-fashioned. Miss Pickerell didn't care. She enjoyed looking up at the carved decorations. Sometimes when she half closed her eyes, they seemed like the faces of quiet children smiling down at her.

"Forevermore!" Miss Pickerell exclaimed suddenly. "I know exactly what I have to do and right this minute. I must go and have my picture taken."

She glanced hastily at her watch. It was 12:30 exactly. Mr. Squeers, the photographer, kept his shop near Square Toe City open until 1:00 on Saturdays. If she hurried, she could just make it. She paused only to grab the knitting bag that she used as a purse and to put on her black felt hat. She attached the hat firmly to her head with two strong hatpins.

"I'll be ready as soon as I take my heavy sweater and my long woolen scarf out of the wardrobe closet downstairs," she told Pumpkins, while they both raced down the stairs. "My umbrella is right in front of the closet."

Professor Humwhistel, Mr. Rugby, and Euphus were in the kitchen now, sitting around the big square table with Miss Lemmon, Mrs. Broadribb, and Mr. Kettelson. Mr. Esticott and Rosemary were there, too. They had just come back, Mr. Esticott explained, from escorting his daughter and her children to the new housing section up the mountain where the inter-county bus stopped.

"I don't approve of women walking alone on unfamiliar streets," he commented to Miss Pickerell. "Anything can happen."

Miss Pickerell did not answer. She was debating with herself about whether or not she should take Nancy Agatha with her. Miss Pickerell seldom went anywhere without her cow and her cat. The cow traveled in the little red trailer with the fringe on top that was attached to the back of the automobile. Pumpkins always sat in the front next to Miss Pickerell and looked out of the window.

"No, I don't think so," Miss Pickerell

decided, talking out loud. "I don't have time to fetch her from the pasture. Actually, I don't even have time to get the automobile out of the barn. And I'm not absolutely sure there will be enough gas in the tank without stopping at the gas station, which would only delay me some more."

"I beg your pardon?" Mr. Esticott, who believed that she was talking to him, asked politely. "I'm not certain that I understand what . . ."

Miss Pickerell waved him aside. A more practical idea was suggesting itself to her. Professor Humwhistel had parked his bicycle next to her front gate. It was a very old bicycle that he used only when his motorcycle had to stay in the mechanic's garage for repairs. But it had brought him up the mountain to the party. And it could take her down to the photography shop.

"Professor Humwhistel," she said, the instant she made up her mind, "I would very much like to borrow your bicycle."

"My . . . my bicycle?" Professor Humwhistel stammered.

"You surely don't mean that," Mrs. Broadribb announced.

"Certainly not," Miss Lemmon echoed.

"I certainly *do*," Miss Pickerell told them. "I need to get down the mountain in a hurry. And I see no reason why I just can't get on the bicycle this minute and go."

"Down the mountain on a Model-T bike!" Mr. Rugby roared.

Miss Pickerell cast him a scornful glance.

"For your information, Mr. Rugby," she said, "my car, which I cannot use at this moment for reasons it would take me too long to explain, is nearly as old as the Model-T automobile you are referring to. And it still gets me where I want to go."

Mr. Rugby looked apologetic.

"I . . . I didn't mean it that way," he sputtered. "And I was wondering, Miss Pickerell, about taking that local bus which starts at the end of your private lane and goes down the . . ."

"That bus, Mr. Rugby," Miss Pickerell replied, cutting him short, "as you should know, since you took it this morning, arrives at the end of my private road every two hours. It will not be there until 1:15. It is also usually late."

She marched over to the wardrobe closet in the little hall that separated the kitchen from her parlor, put on her scarf and her sweater, and hung her big black umbrella over her left arm. Then she adjusted her knitting bag on her right arm and began moving toward the parlor. Rosemary and Euphus, running to keep up with her, giggled. Mr. Esticott, following with Professor Humwhistel, Mr. Kettelson, Mrs. Broadribb, and Miss Lemmon, coughed twice.

"Yes, Mr. Esticott?" Miss Pickerell asked, pausing for an instant. "Did you want to say something?"

"I just wanted to warn you," Mr. Esticott replied. "The roads are still icy in some places."

"I know how to control the brakes on an old bicycle," Miss Pickerell told him.

"It's easy!" Euphus exclaimed. "You just push the pedals counterclockwise."

"Thank you, Euphus," Miss Pickerell said, resuming her march.

Mr. Esticott coughed again. This time, Miss Pickerell did not stop. She went into her parlor.

"Traffic is bad on a Saturday," he called after her. "The cars will get in your way."

"As far as I know, Mr. Esticott," Miss Pickerell said, talking as she walked the length of the parlor, "the horn on the bicycle is in perfect condition. And I don't think I need to tell you that it is easier to get through traffic on a bicycle than with a car."

"I would never do it," Mrs. Broadribb said decisively.

"Absolutely never," Miss Lemmon agreed. "Why, sometimes the cars can't even *see* the bicycles on the road."

"Not see that bicycle?" Rosemary laughed. "Nobody can miss it!"

"That's true," Professor Humwhistel admitted. "I had it painted a bright orange color for exactly that purpose."

He hurried forward in order to open the front door for Miss Pickerell. Mr. Kettelson raced ahead to the gate so that he could lower the bicycle seat. Both Professor Humwhistel and Mr. Kettelson helped her to get on. Miss Pickerell gave her hat a final pat to make sure it was fixed firmly in the middle of her head, placed her glasses a little farther up on her nose, and grasped the handlebars. She was just about to push off when Pumpkins, who had followed her, began to cry. He let out a series of loud piteous meows and looked imploringly up at her.

"Oh, all right," Miss Pickerell said, lean-

31

ing down to lift him into the big straw basket mounted over the front wheel. "I'll take you with me."

And then, her two feet carefully placed on the pedals, her hands tightly gripping the rubber-covered ends of the handlebars, and her red woolen scarf flying behind her, Miss Pickerell, with Pumpkins sitting sideways in the basket, started the ride down the mountain.

3

MISS PICKERELL HAS HER PICTURE TAKEN

The private road which led to the main highway was only partially cleared of snow. Miss Pickerell had spoken twice to the man in the Square Toe City Sanitation Department about it, explaining that she paid a yearly fee for the care of her road and that she expected service in return. But the man had said that the main roads needed to be cleared first. He had promised to send a snow plough up to Square Toe Farm the moment one became available.

"I guess that moment hasn't come yet," Miss Pickerell decided, as she concentrated on weaving the bicycle in between the icy patches and slowly pedaled her way to the intersection. "And he never did say just when it would."

The intersection was the place where she had to make her turn onto the highway. She looked cautiously to the right and to the left, waited for three cars and a small pick-up truck to go whizzing by, and then steered carefully over to the outside lane. She sighed with relief when she saw how clear it was and settled down to steady pedaling. The clock in the tower of the insurance company building opposite Mr. Squeers' place was just striking the hour when she turned off the highway and braked to a stop in front of the photography shop. She dashed over to the bell.

"His radio is going," she said to herself as she waited, "so I'm sure he's inside. And he probably won't mind staying a few extra minutes to take *one* picture."

Mr. Squeers still had on the shirt with the cellophane sleeve cuffs that he wore for work, when he came to answer the bell. He opened his eyes wide when he saw Miss Pickerell.

"Good gracious!" he said, running his fingers through his short gray hair. "Don't tell me you want *another* picture of your cow!"

"Not at all," Miss Pickerell replied stiffly.

"Of your cat then?" the photographer went on. "I see that you have him sitting all ready in the bicycle basket. Well, let me tell you, Miss Pickerell, that cats are very difficult to pose. Unless they are in the mood, they won't sit still and it takes a lot of time to . . ."

"I wish you would listen to me," Miss Pickerell interrupted. "I have no intention of asking you to take a picture of Pumpkins today. I need a photograph of myself. Can you do that?"

Mr. Squeers stared at her through his thick horn-rimmed glasses. He seemed too shocked to open his mouth.

"Certainly," he said finally. "Full-face or profile?"

Miss Pickerell really didn't care. But she had no desire to prolong the conversation.

"Full-face," she said quickly.

"With or without the hat?" Mr. Squeers asked.

"With it," Miss Pickerell told him.

"Well then, come in," Mr. Squeers replied.

Miss Pickerell called out to Pumpkins that she would be back very soon and entered the waiting room. There were even more pictures than usual on the wall, she noticed.

Many of them were photos of school graduates, dressed in their best and holding their diplomas so everybody could see them. A doorway with a purple curtain across it blocked off the studio where Mr. Squeers took his pictures. He swished the curtain aside and escorted Miss Pickerell to a chair.

"If you would like to rearrange your hair or anything like that," he said, "the mirror is to your left."

"That won't be necessary," Miss Pickerell said, sitting down. "I am ready."

Mr. Squeers leaned over the chair and scrutinized her face.

"I hope you won't mind my saying this, Miss Pickerell," he commented, "but I don't approve of your hat."

"There is nothing wrong with my hat," Miss Pickerell retorted instantly. "It is warm and serviceable and it . . ."

"Frankly," Mr. Squeers, still examining her, interrupted, "I'd prefer something with a little more style. A flower perhaps on the brim. Or even a feather or a . . ."

"Pooh!" Miss Pickerell exclaimed.

"And I don't believe," Mr. Squeers went on, "that the hat should sit quite so squarely on your head. Tilted a little to the right, maybe. . . . What do you think, Miss Pickerell?"

Miss Pickerell gave her hatpins two swift jabs to make sure the hat stayed exactly where she had put it and said, "Please go on with your picture-taking, Mr. Squeers."

The photographer moved back to the

wooden stand on which his camera rested. He placed a large black cloth over his head, told her to smile, and clicked the camera twice.

"I will have two proofs to show you in a few minutes," he said, taking the cloth off his head and withdrawing behind the door that led to his darkroom.

Miss Pickerell waited until his footsteps had definitely retreated. Then she walked rapidly over to the mirror. She pushed her hat a little to one side and looked critically at the effect. She set it straight again the moment she heard Mr. Squeers returning.

"I would recommend the first proof," he stated, as he handed it to her. "I would also suggest, if I may say so, touching it up here and there."

"Touching it up?" Miss Pickerell repeated.

"To take the fatigue lines out," Mr. Squeers explained. "Those lines around the eyes, for example. They seem especially bad. And near the forehead here, above the . . ."

"I wouldn't dream of it!" Miss Pickerell said immediately. "No touching up!"

"Movie stars do it all the time," Mr.

Squeers argued. "Why, only the other day I saw a picture of that television star, the one who used to play in the Wednesday afternoon special, and I know for a fact that . . ."

"Movie stars have face lifts, too," Miss Pickerell said sharply. "And I have no intention of having *that* done, either! I will need fifty copies of the photograph, Mr. Squeers. When can you have them ready?"

"A week from today," Mr. Squeers said, writing the order down in his little book.

"Thank you," Miss Pickerell replied. "If you would like me to leave a small deposit, I . . ."

"I don't believe so," Mr. Squeers answered.

He held the curtain aside again when Miss Pickerell began to leave and he walked with her into the waiting room.

"I would think twice about the touching up," he said earnestly. "Or I would have another picture taken, some time when you look a little better. Are you sure, Miss Pickerell, that you are not coming down with something?"

"Coming down with what?" Miss Pickerell asked.

"Well," Mr. Squeers said, "it can be any

number of things. That terrible influenza, perhaps, that almost everybody has had this winter. I myself had a bout a few weeks ago. It came on just like that and lasted for . . ."

Miss Pickerell paused to check on possible symptoms. Her nose wasn't running. Her throat didn't feel scratchy. She felt no muscle pains in her joints, no soreness, either.

"I am in perfect health, Mr. Squeers," she told the photographer. "I may be a little exhausted from the surprise Valentine's Day party I had this morning, but . . ."

"Yes, yes," Mr. Squeers said hastily. "I wanted so much to come. But, as you can see, the sign on my door says, OPEN UNTIL ONE O'CLOCK. I couldn't get away. You will excuse me, I sincerely hope, Miss Pickerell."

Miss Pickerell nodded and made her way to the door. Mr. Squeers' radio was just starting the 1:30 news when she walked out to the sidewalk. She could hear the announcer talking breathlessly about still another oil spill as she waved to Pumpkins and headed for Professor Humwhistel's bicycle.

4
OFF TO THE THREE CHIMNEY LODGE

The road back up the mountain to Square Toe Farm seemed to Miss Pickerell to be much more difficult. She had a problem with her breathing from the very beginning. Twice, she actually had to steer the bicycle off the road and rest for a while.

"It's this unseasonable weather," she complained to Pumpkins the second time. "The month of February is not *supposed* to be hot."

Just after the intersection leading to her private lane, she stopped again. She took off her sweater and tied it around her neck by the long, floppy sleeves. She took off her scarf too and stuffed it into her knitting bag.

"I'll feel a lot better now," she told herself comfortingly.

But she saw that even Pumpkins noticed how she panted all the way to the farmyard gate. He turned around in his basket to look questioningly up at her.

"Maybe I really *am* coming down with something," she said to him, as they climbed the back stairs together. "It might not be a bad idea to take my temperature."

She walked past Euphus and Rosemary, who were now alone in the kitchen. Rosemary called out that she was just making a drawing for a MISS PICKERELL FAN CLUB button and that she would show it to Miss Pickerell as soon as the design was ready.

"Good!" Miss Pickerell told her from the wardrobe closet where she was depositing her sweater and her umbrella.

She pressed the back of her hand against her forehead on the way up to her bedroom. The skin felt quite cool. She decided not to bother with the thermometer.

"There's nothing the matter with me," she said out loud. "Nothing except nerves. And that's Mr. Squeers' doing. Silly man with all that nonsense about fatigue lines and face lifts!"

She moved toward the bureau and gazed at herself in the broad framed mirror that hung above it. She paid special attention to her hat.

"I probably *would* look better in a new one," she remarked to her reflection. "Maybe something with a ribbon on it, a red one perhaps, to give me a little color."

She took the hat off, peered at her face carefully, and sighed.

"No," she said sadly. "A hat won't help. Perhaps a permanent wave. Mrs. Broadribb is always getting one of those."

The mental vision of the stiff ridges and the mountains of curls in Mrs. Broadribb's hair was enough to make her give up that idea immediately, however. Her thoughts turned to Rosemary and her new blow-dry cut. It was short and easy to take care of and . . .

"Ridiculous!" Miss Pickerell exclaimed. "What *can* I be thinking of?"

She looked into the mirror again. The fatigue lines that Mr. Squeers had mentioned were unmistakeably present. So were some tight worry lines around her mouth that he had not noticed. Or if he had noticed, he hadn't said anything about them.

"What I need," Miss Pickerell concluded, talking out loud again, "is a vacation. A nice quiet vacation away from surprise parties

and oil spills and supertankers, away even from Pumpkins and Nancy Agatha. I need to be by myself and think of *nothing*."

She sat down on the edge of her bed and gave the matter some further consideration. She had taken that kind of vacation once, she remembered. It was after her trip to the moon. She had been very tired and the rest in the small hotel had worked wonders for her.

"Now, what was the name of that place?" she mused. "I know it was near the ocean. And I'm sure it was a long brown house with elm trees growing on either side of the doorway and three big red chimneys on the roof."

She jumped up suddenly, startling Pumpkins out of the face wash he was giving himself on top of the bureau.

"Of course!" she exclaimed. "It was the Three Chimney Lodge in Chickam County. I'll go call them up."

Euphus and Rosemary listened to every word when Miss Pickerell picked up the kitchen telephone and asked the operator to connect her with the Three Chimney Lodge. They stared when she said, "Yes, Mr. Lovelace, I understand perfectly. There are trains leaving the Square Toe City depot at 4:30 p.m., 6:30 p.m., and 10:30 p.m. daily. And you do have a room available. Yes, I'll call when I decide to come and someone can meet me at the train when I get there. Thank you, Mr. Lovelace. Thank you very much."

"You're going on a vacation!" Rosemary shouted the minute Miss Pickerell hung up the receiver.

"I didn't say that," Miss Pickerell retorted.

"Well, you should," Rosemary replied. "You need one."

"Do I?" Miss Pickerell, reminded again of the fatigue lines, asked thoughtfully.

"I'll help you pack," Rosemary volunteered, rushing over to the wardrobe closet and pulling out Miss Pickerell's worn cardboard valise. "And I do wish you'd get yourself a new suitcase."

Miss Pickerell looked past the wardrobe closet to the little hall where Professor Humwhistel and Mr. Esticott were now quietly sitting on the horsehair sofa. Professor Humwhistel was nodding his head. Mr. Kettelson was staring down at the fringes of the carpet runner that lay under the sofa. She turned back to fix her eyes on Rosemary again.

"I *certainly* did not say I was going on a vacation *today*," she told her.

"It's a good time to go," Professor Humwhistel said slowly. "The weather is exceptionally warm and . . ."

"Warm enough for summer dresses," Rosemary exclaimed. "I'll run up to the bedroom and get them."

"I'll call Mr. Lovelace," Euphus shouted,

skidding across the newly waxed kitchen floor to the telephone. "I'll tell him you're taking the 4:30 train."

Miss Pickerell was sure she was going to develop a splitting headache at any moment. This commotion was even worse than the fuss at the Valentine's Day party. She walked over to the sofa to sit down beside Professor Humwhistel and Mr. Kettelson.

"And," Professor Humwhistel said, continuing with the sentence he had left off, "and I don't believe you will need to worry about your animals." He smiled at Mr. Kettelson.

"No," Mr. Kettelson said, raising his eyes immediately from the carpet runner fringe. "I will be most happy to stay on the farm and take care of Pumpkins and Nancy Agatha. My assistant can easily manage the shop for me. Actually, I was just thinking that I don't really need a full-time assistant. I was turning over in my mind the idea of discharging him after our next sale. I . . ."

"Thank you, Mr. Kettelson," interrupted Miss Pickerell, who had heard all of this before. "I can go with an easy mind if I know that you are with my animals."

Rosemary began packing the things she

had brought down from the bedroom. She raced up again for the letter paper when Miss Pickerell told her she was planning to write all her thank-you notes during her stay at the Three Chimney Lodge. Mr. Kettelson ran out to get the automobile and the trailer and to bring Nancy Agatha down from the pasture. Professor Humwhistel followed Miss Pickerell back into the kitchen. Euphus was still talking on the telephone. He lowered his voice when Miss Pickerell walked over to take an extra heavy sweater out of the closet.

"Just in case the weather changes," she explained to Professor Humwhistel. "It's better to be prepared."

Professor Humwhistel nodded.

"Where," he asked absently, "where did you say you were going, Miss Pickerell? I'm afraid I didn't hear the name."

"To the Three Chimney Lodge in Chickam," Miss Pickerell said. "The winter rates are so cheap, I may even stay for a week."

"Chickam! Chickam!" Professor Humwhistel repeated. "It sounds a little familiar. Unfortunately, I can't recall exactly in what connection."

-    "It will come to you," Miss Pickerell told him.

"I believe it was important," Professor Humwhistel murmured. "Quite important. I'm trying to think . . ."

Miss Pickerell turned away from him to look at her kitchen clock. The bright yellow hands stood at ten minutes to three.

"There'll be time enough for me to stop for some gas if I need any," she said to herself, as she folded her sweater over her arm and examined her knitting bag to make sure she had her wallet, her extra pair of glasses, the scarf she was knitting, and Euphus's list of names and addresses. She added the letter paper that Rosemary had handed her. She raised her eyebrows when Rosemary objected that the heavy sweater was plain unnecessary in such warm weather.

"It will probably get cold at night," she told her firmly.

"It won't," Rosemary announced. "I just heard the extended weather outlook. Tomorrow will be even hotter. The day after, too."

Rosemary leaned down over the valise to place two checked cotton dresses and one striped summer suit on top. And, as Miss Pickerell gasped, she crawled along the bottom of the closet and came out lugging a bulky canvas bag marked TO MISS PICKERELL, FROM HER ADMIRING FRIENDS AT THE OCEANOGRAPHIC INSTITUTE. MORE HAPPY SCUBA EXPEDITIONS!

"I have no intention of doing any scuba diving in the middle of February," Miss Pickerell said, shuddering.

"You may change your mind," Rosemary

replied, quickly closing the suitcase and handing it together with the canvas bag to Professor Humwhistel to carry out. "And don't forget, I'm putting some peanut butter and tomato sandwiches in with your knitting."

Euphus and Rosemary were the first ones to get into the trailer with Nancy Agatha. Mr. Kettelson moved in beside them. Professor Humwhistel sat next to Miss Pickerell. Pumpkins snuggled on Miss Pickerell's lap. All the way to the train station, she assured him that Mr. Kettelson would take good care of him and Nancy Agatha. She said the same thing to the cow when she kissed her goodbye at the depot.

The train was puffing gently into the station as Professor Humwhistel, Euphus, and Rosemary walked down the stairs to the platform with Miss Pickerell. Mr. Kettelson remained behind to watch Pumpkins and Nancy Agatha.

"Listen, Aunt Lavinia," Euphus screamed, when the porter had deposited the luggage and Miss Pickerell stood near the door, waving goodbye. "Listen to what we arranged over the telephone!"

The voices of the junior members of THE MISS PICKERELL FAN CLUB, SQUARE TOE

, rang out from the front end of the platform.

"Miss Pickerell, Miss Pickerell," they sang,
"our hearts you fill with pride,
We wish you good health
and fun at the blue seaside."

"I'll write to you," Miss Pickerell told them, as she waved more vigorously than ever. "I promise. I . . ."

And then, just as the train was starting to pull out, Professor Humwhistel shouted up to her, "I remember! I remember now, Miss Pickerell!"

He ran alongside the train to finish what he was saying.

"Chickam! Chickam!" he shouted. "I believe it may well be the place that Mr. Rugby's customer . . ."

The train picked up speed. If Professor Humwhistel ever finished his sentence, Miss Pickerell did not hear it.

5

THE MYSTERIOUS
MR. LOVELACE

There were plenty of empty seats on the train and Miss Pickerell was able to make herself comfortable. She deposited her umbrella and her sweater on the overhead rack where the porter had placed her suitcase and her scuba bag. Then she put her knitting bag down on the vacant seat next to her, and stretched her feet out so that they could rest on the two unoccupied seats facing her. The imitation leather seat covers were already so dirty, she didn't think her shoes could possibly make them any worse. But after a moment's further deliberation, she changed her mind and carefully spread her large white cotton handkerchief under the shoes.

"I suppose I should eat something," she said, when she settled herself back again and began to rummage around in her knitting bag.

The sandwiches, neatly wrapped in waxed paper, were on the bottom. Miss Pickerell dug them out and sighed.

"I guess I'm not as crazy about peanut butter and tomato sandwiches as Rosemary is," she reflected, as she put them aside.

Rosemary had slipped the very latest issue of THE LADIES' AND GENTS' NEEDLE-CRAFT MAGAZINE into the knitting bag, too. Miss Pickerell looked eagerly at the patterns and stitches suggested for bedspreads, fancy pillow cases, and leggings for younger children. None of the patterns appealed to her, and besides she knew most of the stitches by heart. She turned to the *Swapper's Column* at the back of the magazine. The only offer appearing today was a man who wanted to exchange fifty jigsaw puzzles of nature scenes for fifty jigsaw puzzles of city life. Miss Pickerell put the magazine away and looked out of the dusty window.

"It needs a good wash," she commented to the woman conductor who came toward her with the tickets. "Personally, I would use ammonia with the water."

The woman conductor collected the money for the ticket, gave her skirt, with the coins jingling in the pockets, a weary tug, and said nothing. Miss Pickerell turned back to the window.

They were passing a small town now. The train was moving slowly and Miss Pickerell could see the slushy streets and people trudging through the slush and gazing unbelievingly up at the blazing sun. A man in front of a dry goods store was removing the melting snow from his sidewalk. A small boy in a bright green stocking cap was trying to climb up a soft snow pile and sliding down instead. Miss Pickerell was just looking back to see whether he had hurt himself when the train gave a sudden lurch and started to pick up speed again. They were moving into open country where snow banks still lined the sides of the roadbed. Hurtling between them, the train blew the snow into clouds of powdery flakes that landed on the window pane and stayed there.

"Oh, dear!" Miss Pickerell exclaimed, distastefully examining the peanut butter and tomato sandwiches again and deciding that she would go hunt up a snack bar.

She found one in the very next car. It looked most inviting, with a coffee pot, tea kettle, and a round saucepan all bubbling on a little electric stove and yellow plastic

spoons and cups stacked next to the cakes
and sandwiches in their cellophane envelopes. A young man with a snub nose and
freckles stood behind the counter. He had
his elbows propped up on it and was reading from a thick book that lay open in front
of him. Miss Pickerell coughed to get his
attention.

"Oh, excuse me," he said politely. "I . . .
I sometimes get so interested in what I'm
reading, I forget everything else. My boss,
Mr. Esticott, occasionally has to speak to me
about this. I'm Mortimor Tooting and I'm
here to serve you."

Miss Pickerell told him her own name and added that Mr. Esticott was a friend of hers. Then she peered down to see what Mortimor Tooting was reading.

"It's my book on microbiology," he explained. "I'm studying all about it at the university. I go to school at night and work during the day and on weekends so that I can help my parents pay the university fees. They're very high these days."

Miss Pickerell thought the young man was definitely doing the right thing and told him so. She also told him that she had a nephew who was especially interested in science.

"Euphus was writing only this morning about oil-eating microbes," she said. "He was doing his science homework."

Mortimor Tooting turned some pages in his book.

"It says here," he commented, "that the oil-eating microbes are not completely effective. They don't work on all the oil components."

"Oh?" exclaimed Miss Pickerell.

"Well," the young man went on, "they're supposed to break down or, as some people say, to eat up the oil components."

"The oil components?" Miss Pickerell repeated.

"Yes," Mortimor told her. "You see, crude oil is a mixture of many different hydrocarbons."

"I know about those," Miss Pickerell said, remembering that she had once looked it up in the H volume of her encyclopedia. "Hydrocarbons are a combination of hydrogen and carbons."

"Exactly," Mortimor Tooting agreed, while he turned more pages in his book. "There are aromatic hydrocarbons and aliphatic hydrocarbons and cycloparaffinic hydrocarbons and . . ."

He looked up from the book and laughed.

"Anyway," he said, "I guess the microbes are picky eaters. They refuse to break down all the components."

"I see," Miss Pickerell nodded, though she was not entirely sure that she did.

Mortimor closed his book, took a deep breath, and scrutinized Miss Pickerell cautiously.

"Would it surprise you," he asked, "to hear that scientists are now contemplating the use of laboratory-bred microbes that will eat everything we want them to?"

Miss Pickerell was about to say "Pooh!" but thought better of it when she recalled all the words she hadn't even understood in Euphus's science homework. She planned to consult her encyclopedia about them as soon as she got home. She would also look up the long words Mr. Tooting had just used about the hydrocarbons. There was clearly a lot she didn't know about science.

"What do you need to breed these new microbes?" she inquired respectfully.

Mortimor shook his head sadly.

"I know we need the bacteria and the fungi," he replied, "but I don't know what else. The idea is so new, it isn't even in my textbook yet. My microbiology professor says the scientists are still testing the theory out in the laboratory."

"Well," Miss Pickerell said heatedly, "I wish they'd come out of their laboratories and start testing it in the real world! When I hear about the oil spills and what the oil contamination does to sea birds and . . ."

She pushed the nightmarish thought out of her head and tried to concentrate on the sandwiches in front of her. Mortimor Tooting looked at them too.

"I would really recommend the corn chowder," he said, pouring some out of the round saucepan. "It's piping hot and very tasty."

He poured some for himself too and offered Miss Pickerell a stool behind the counter.

"Are you off on a winter vacation?" he asked between careful sips of the steaming chowder.

"Only for a few days," Miss Pickerell told him. "To the Three Chimney Lodge in Chickam."

"The Three Chimney Lodge!" Mortimor Tooting sputtered, nearly choking on the sip he had not quite finished swallowing.

"I beg your pardon?" Miss Pickerell asked.

Mortimor put his cup of chowder down, raised his arms over his head to help him catch his breath, and looked thoughtfully at Miss Pickerell.

"I hope you like mysteries," he said, "because you're certainly going to meet one at the Three Chimney Lodge."

"You must be mistaken," Miss Pickerell told him. "I've been to the Three Chimney Lodge before and . . ."

"Before Mr. Lovelace bought it," Mortimor broke in. "Before the mysterious Mr. Lovelace moved in and began pacing the floors and following people around and throwing some of them out and . . ."

"Something must be worrying him," Miss Pickerell suggested, recalling that she often marched up and down her kitchen floor when she had a problem on her mind. She couldn't remember ever having followed anyone around, though, and she had *never* thrown anybody out of her house, even when she had been very sorely tempted to do so. There was the time when Mrs. Broadribb . . .

"Something certainly *is* worrying him," Mortimor Tooting went on insistently. "He wasn't too bad when he first took over the hotel, but lately . . . he's . . . he's as nervous as a cat."

"Not all cats are nervous," Miss Pickerell said instantly. "My own cat, Pumpkins, who knows how much he is loved, is not nervous at all."

Mortimor frowned. He also clasped and unclasped his hand on the end of his spoon.

"You don't realize how serious this is, Miss Pickerell," he said. "Mr. Esticott and I met there for lunch between trips last week and we actually saw him throw a lady guest out of the parlor because she was watching television. Then he came back and took the set out of the room."

"Mercy!" Miss Pickerell exclaimed, while she reviewed in her head a few of the programs she had seen and felt some of her sympathies going out to the mysterious Mr. Lovelace.

"And Mr. Esticott believes," Mortimor continued, "that this Mr. Lovelace is easily the most nervous man he has ever seen. Mr. Esticott even went so far as to say the nervousness might be bordering on insanity."

Miss Pickerell didn't have a very high opinion of Mr. Esticott's ability to diagnose insanity. Why, he couldn't even recognize how very nervous he himself was! But she decided not to discuss this with the young man. After all, Mr. Esticott was the chief conductor and Mortimor Tooting was only a café car attendant.

"Well," she said, "I don't imagine your Mr. Lovelace will get very upset with me. I'll be spending most of my time knitting. After I finish writing some thank-you notes, that is. Then I'll take a walk on the beach. And then, I'll probably be ready to come home."

She sighed, thinking of Pumpkins and Nancy Agatha and already regretting that she hadn't brought them along.

The train was starting to slow down. Up front, the engineer was sounding a long, drawn out whistle. In the next car the woman conductor was walking along the aisle announcing the next station.

"We'll be pulling into Chickam in a few minutes," Mortimor Tooting said. "I'll take your luggage off for you."

He put her knitting bag, her scuba bag, her umbrella, and her suitcase with her sweater on top of it out on the platform and helped her across the space that separated the platform from the train.

"It was nice talking to you, Miss Pickerell," he said as he walked back up the train steps. "Have a good time! And whatever you do, don't get that insane Mr. Lovelace into one of his rages."

"Heavens!" Miss Pickerell said, smiling. "I wouldn't dream of it!"

6

THIRTEEN AT THE DINNER TABLE

Miss Pickerell was the only passenger to get off at Chickam. And there was only one person waiting near the station, a lanky young woman with bright red hair who stood outside a battered station wagon. She ran over to Miss Pickerell immediately.

"You're Miss Pickerell, aren't you?" she asked, giving her a very cheerful smile. "I'm Mrs. Lovelace. How nice that the train was on schedule! If I drive fast, I can still get you to the Three Chimney Lodge in time for dinner."

Miss Pickerell shuddered. She didn't believe in fast driving. Personally, she made it a practice never to drive her own automobile more than thirty-five miles an hour. But she said nothing and followed Mrs. Lovelace into the station wagon.

Mrs. Lovelace steered the car across the

bumpy railroad bridge, screeched past a school yard, a trolley barn, a pickle factory, and a glassworks shop in Chickam, and made a sharp turn down a country lane which wound between snow-flecked hedges on either side. It was twenty minutes after seven but there was still enough light for Miss Pickerell to notice an exceptionally tall, dark-haired man disappear into the shadows of a clump of pine trees. What startled Miss Pickerell was that he seemed to be carrying a number of large dead birds by

their legs in one hand and a long-handled shovel in the other. Miss Pickerell wondered about this while she clung to the edge of her seat and kept pressing her right foot down in an imaginary braking motion. She calmed down a little when Mrs. Lovelace turned on the headlights and reduced her speed to proceed along a narrow gravel path that was overhung with branches of maple trees just coming into leaf. The path led to the house where Mrs. Lovelace drew up in front of the two gnarled elm trees that Miss Pickerell remembered from her last visit. Off to the left was the old barn that she had wanted to explore but hadn't gotten to the last time. A light from a small window high up in the barn revealed a very bare lawn. Miss Pickerell was just getting ready to make a strong recommendation for fertilizer when Mrs. Lovelace, carrying the suitcase, the scuba bag, and the umbrella, bounced out of the car.

"You can really smell the fresh air here," she said, sniffing twice, while she opened a door that had little blue lights running across the top. "I'm sure that will give you a good appetite for dinner."

The dining room was straight ahead and

to the rear of the entrance hall at the Three Chimney Lodge. It was large and square and had a rubber plant standing in a brass pot in the far right corner. The long table filled the middle of the room. Four ladies sat on the left-hand side. Mrs. Lovelace introduced them as the sisters Loretta, Coretta, and Floretta Frowley, who were on a weekend holiday from the glassworks shop, and Mrs. Gladys Goodbody, the town organist. She also introduced Mr. and Mrs. John Slitherspoon, year-round residents at the Three Chimney Lodge, and the five men who sat with them on the opposite side of the table. Mr. Beadle, Mr. Deacon, Mr. Fiedler, Mr. Heating, and Mr. Jeetowitz, Junior, each got up in turn and shook hands with Miss Pickerell. Mr. Jeetowitz, Junior, explained that the pickle factory where he worked was shut down because of a combined strike and anti-union bomb scare, added that he would probably remain at the Lodge for an indefinite time, and ended up by murmuring, "What is this world coming too?" Miss Pickerell did not give him any answer.

She followed Mrs. Lovelace around to her right and into the kitchen where she washed her hands at the sink and stopped to straighten her hat and to drape her sweater around her shoulders. She returned to the dining room and sat down between Mr. and Mrs. Slitherspoon.

"I hope you don't mind thirteen at the dinner table, Miss Pickerell," Mrs. Lovelace, seated directly across from her, laughed. "My husband will be in shortly."

"I mind," Mr. Slitherspoon, a round little man with a neat white beard, replied, as he headed for the kitchen. "I hope, however, that the dinner will make up for it. Thank you for letting me prepare it, Mrs. Lovelace."

"He's a retired chef," Mrs. Slitherspoon, who was even rounder and much larger than Mr. Slitherspoon, explained. "He used to make wonderful dishes. But, lately . . ."

She sighed and went out to help Mr. Slitherspoon bring in the meal. She pushed the centerpiece of mixed chrysanthemums and snapdragons aside to make room for the huge bowl he placed on the table.

"My own kind of variety salad," he announced.

"His own kind of health food," Mrs. Slitherspoon laughed.

Miss Pickerell agreed that the salad certainly had variety when she tried it. She was able to identify squash, onions, cucumbers, beets, and parsnips in the mixture that Mr. Slitherspoon had thrown together and then seasoned with some very mild horseradish. It all tasted delicious, and as she drank the ice cold cider that Mr. Slitherspoon said should be sipped with it she looked forward to exchanging recipes with him.

But she blinked when she saw the dessert. It consisted of yeast tablets, smeared with cream cheese and served with a big grape on each tablet.

"He has bottles and bottles of them," Mrs. Slitherspoon leaned over to confide to her. "And bunches and bunches of . . ."

The sudden slamming of the outside door and the sound of rapid footsteps cut Mrs. Slitherspoon short. Miss Pickerell looked up to see a tall thin man with very black hair and dark eyes deeply sunk in his head approach the table. He was wearing snow boots and a leather jacket with torn cuffs and was carrying a pile of unevenly folded newspapers in his arms. For a moment, Miss Pickerell thought he looked familiar. She had seen him someplace, but

. . . but where? Mrs. Lovelace's voice broke in on her uneasy speculations.

"My husband," Mrs. Lovelace said, "Mr. Angus Lovelace. And this is our newest visitor to the Three Chimney Lodge, Miss Lavinia Pickerell."

Mr. Lovelace made no comment. His eyes darted restlessly around the table and settled for a moment on his wife. With what seemed to Miss Pickerell a small nod, he then walked past the rubber plant and into the kitchen. Through the half-open door, she could see him stuffing newspapers into the shining black coal stove. He used a piece of kindling to stir up the coals. Then he blew into the belly of the stove to coax the hot ashes into a flame.

Miss Pickerell looked away when she felt the hard stare of someone watching her. She wheeled around in time to catch Mrs. Lovelace's searching gaze. There was fear in Mrs. Lovelace's eyes, she noticed, and cold suspicion. But the smile took the place of the stare almost instantly. She threw bright glances at everybody when she got up from the table.

"Do join us in the parlor," she said to Miss Pickerell. "Mrs. Goodbody has kindly consented to entertain us with some musical pieces on the piano. She plays the piano almost as beautifully as she does the organ. Isn't that so, Mrs. Goodbody?"

Miss Pickerell declined politely. She had some letters to write, she explained, and would go directly to her room.

Mr. Lovelace carried her suitcase, scuba bag, and umbrella upstairs. He opened the door for her and handed her a key without saying a word.

"That *is* a strange man," Miss Pickerell reflected, as she stood in the doorway remembering Mortimor Tooting's warning and listening to the strains of *Home on the Range* that were drifting up from the parlor. "I'm not sure about Mrs. Lovelace, either. Not at all sure!"

She forgot all about her doubts when she began to examine her room. The bed that stood against the side wall had plain white sheets on it. They gave off a faint scent of the outdoors where, Miss Pickerell realized, they had probably been hung to dry. The towels in the adjoining bathroom had the same fresh smell. And the bathtub was the kind that she especially liked, a large high one set firmly on stout, sensible legs. She was also glad to see that the floor under the tub had been swept out thoroughly, that there was not a speck of dust anywhere, and that her bedroom window was open exactly the right amount from the top.

"I'll be just fine here," she told herself happily, as she unpacked and put some of her things into the dark wooden dresser and arranged her dresses and scuba equipment in a closet that was neatly lined with cedar paneling.

She got into bed with her box of letter paper, her new ball-point pen, and Euphus's list of names and addresses placed conveniently at her elbow. The lamp on the night table next to the bed gave off a small light that was just right.

"And I'll be able to do a lot of this writing tonight," she promised herself. "I'm not the least bit sleepy. I'll start with the envelopes."

But the pen slipped out of her hand the minute her head touched the plump, goose-down pillows. She reached over to switch off the lamp, stretched herself out more comfortably, and listened to the wind beating against the window pane.

"It must be the north wind," she mur-

mured drowsily, pulling the warm comfort-
er up under her chin. "The north wind
coming up from the sea. . . ."

She fell asleep with the sound of the
ocean waves rumbling, a little like far-away
thunder, in and around her ears.

7

THE SHIP AT THE OCEAN FRONT

"Mercy!" Miss Pickerell exclaimed the next morning when she got ready to call up her farm and ask about her cow and her cat. "I'd forgotten that there were no telephones in the bedrooms here. I'll just have to use the one downstairs."

She dressed quickly, slung her umbrella and her knitting bag over her arm, and crossed the hall to the staircase. She breathed a sigh of relief when she reached the bottom of the stairs and saw that the telephone was not in use. It stood on the long narrow counter opposite the front door and a little to the left of the staircase. Mr. Lovelace sat in back of the counter and in front of a row of letter boxes hanging on the wall. He said she could use the telephone and that he would add the cost of the call to her bill. Miss Pickerell dialed the number after she signed the guest book and handed Mr. Lovelace her key to put in her box.

The connection she made with Square Toe Farm was not a very good one. She had to ask Mr. Kettelson to talk louder when he told her about how he milked Nancy Agatha and kept her in the upper pasture where it was sunnier and about how Pumpkins followed him around every minute.

"But what I really want to tell you about," he said after that, "is Mr. Esticott. He called me this morning to say he is definitely of the opinion that you should come home immediately. He doesn't believe all this traveling around is good for you."

Miss Pickerell nearly sputtered with indignation.

"I don't see that my comings and goings are any concern of Mr. Esticott's," she replied. "This is a free country and I have every right to . . ."

"You don't understand," Mr. Kettelson interrupted. "A young man by the name of Mortimor Tooting called Mr. Esticott yesterday and explained some things to him."

"I never heard of such nonsense!" Miss Pickerell replied promptly.

"Mr. Esticott is under the impression," Mr. Kettelson continued, "that you may be in considerable danger."

"I am in no danger whatsoever," Miss Pickerell said, almost shouting.

"And if I am any judge, Miss Pickerell," Mr. Kettelson persisted, "there is a great deal more trouble to come."

"What trouble?" she asked, actually shouting this time and nearly putting down the receiver.

"You realize, of course, Miss Pickerell," Mr. Kettelson said, raising his voice too, "that we have your best interests at heart, Mr. Esticott and I, and that . . ."

"Yes, yes," Miss Pickerell assured him. "Thank you very much, Mr. Kettelson."

She was nearly fuming when she turned away from the telephone. The way Mr. Lovelace kept his eyes fixed steadily on her didn't calm her down any, either.

"Breakfast is served in the coffee lounge," he said stiffly, while he drummed his long, thin fingers restlessly on the desk blotter and continued to look at her. "Around the hall leading from the far end of the dining room."

"I see," Miss Pickerell said, swallowing her instant impulse to ask him why he found it necessary to examine her so closely and walking instead into and through the dining room.

The sight of the coffee lounge revived her good spirits a little. It faced a sunny lawn and had small white tables, covered with pretty pink and white cloths scattered around. Mrs. Lovelace, her hair tied back with a wide red ribbon, stood stooping over a corner buffet table, buttering thick slices of bread.

"Good morning, Miss Pickerell," she called out. "I see you are an early riser. Not like any of our other guests. Come and help yourself to some breakfast."

Miss Pickerell put orange juice, coffee, and two pieces of the buttered bread on her tray. Mrs. Lovelace said this was not enough and added a large boiled egg, a bowl of cereal, and a rolled-up napkin containing a knife, a fork, and three spoons. Miss Pickerell carried the tray to a table near a window. The window was a broad one and looked directly out on the lawn.

"This must be the back of the house," Miss Pickerell said to herself, as she deposited her umbrella and her knitting bag on the windowsill, settled herself in her chair, and began sipping her orange juice. "Yes, I'm sure it is because the hall leading into the coffee lounge is in the opposite direction from the entrance hall. I don't think I ever did get the geography of this place straight."

Feeling relieved about knowing exactly where she was at the moment, she tapped with a spoon on the shell of her egg and took another look at the lawn. It bordered on the gravel drive that wound around the house. A narrow sandy path intersected it on the other side.

"And that path leads down to the ocean," she said, half out loud. "I remember *that* distinctly. Yes, I can even see the ocean from here. But why does it have such a muddy look on this bright sunny day?"

She bit into a piece of bread, thought of how glad she was that Rosemary had packed her summer dresses, and watched two sandpipers and a tern shivering and picking at their feathers where they stood on patches of melting snow on the lawn. The feathers seemed to be glued together with mud, a strange mud that shone unnaturally in the sunshine. Miss Pickerell jumped out of her chair when one of the sandpipers, making a desperate effort to fly, tried to stretch out his wings and fell right down.

"Forevermore!" she burst out. "What can be the matter with him?"

It was when she was peering out of the window for another look that she noticed something jutting out of the ocean. The shape made her think of the big radio

antenna that Euphus had rigged up in his
back yard. On second thought, she decided
that it was more like the radar equipment
she had seen that time when she rescued
her rocks from a sunken cargo ship. The
ship's antenna had stuck up out of the water
and . . .

Miss Pickerell froze. She knew suddenly
what Professor Humwhistel had been trying
to tell her when he ran after the train and
why Mr. Esticott and Mortimor Tooting
found Mr. Lovelace acting so strangely, and
why he, Mr. Lovelace, simply *had* to take out

the television set and to throw the daily newspaper into the coal stove.

"It's the tanker," she whispered, as she reached for her umbrella and her knitting bag and then sat down again. "It's the supertanker with the oil spill that Mr. Rugby's customer mentioned. The dark look on the water is from the oil. And the tern and the sandpipers are soaked with the same oil. Oh my, oh my, oh my!"

She shuddered as she stared long and thoughtfully at the birds.

"No," she said to all the terrible doubts and anxieties that were insistently coming into her head. "No, I will *not* go away and find a really quiet place for my vacation. I *care* for these creatures. And if I care, I have to do something to help. I'll go take a look at that tanker. After that, I'll do what I *have* to do."

She nearly bumped into Mr. and Mrs. Lovelace as she hurried across the coffee lounge. Mrs. Lovelace was standing now with her back to the door. Mr. Lovelace, tall and erect behind her, completely blocked the way out.

"Going somewhere, Miss Pickerell?" he asked icily.

"For a walk," Miss Pickerell answered, saying the first thing that came into her head.

"Chickam makes a nice walk," Mrs. Lovelace said very fast. "It's only a mile away. Our two antique shops there are open on Sundays and our new rock band gives free concerts at the . . ."

Miss Pickerell was barely listening. The muscles in Mr. Lovelace's lean face were twitching and the look in his dark, deep-set eyes was sending shivers up and down her spine. She tried to ignore them and to take a strong hold on herself.

"Thank you for your suggestion, Mrs. Lovelace," she said.

Mr. Lovelace moved closer to her.

"I doubt very much that Miss Pickerell is planning to visit an antique shop," he said, leaning down to stare directly into her eyes.

Miss Pickerell stared back. Her heart was thumping wildly. But she was going to come right to the point. There was no other way, she decided.

"No," she said, "I am not going to visit an antique shop. I am walking down to the ocean to take a good look at that oil tanker."

Mr. Lovelace leaned all the way down. He

laughed out loud. To Miss Pickerell, it sounded more like a snarl.

"I thought," he said, "I thought that was what your friend was warning you about over the telephone."

"You listened," Miss Pickerell snapped, practically bristling at this outrage. "You intruded on my privacy."

"I couldn't help overhearing," Mr. Lovelace replied. "I apologize."

"Thank you," Miss Pickerell said. "I'm glad that, at least, you have good manners. But for your information, I want to tell you that my friend said nothing of the sort. I saw the tanker plainly from the coffee lounge windows. I even saw the oil that . . ."

"No one else has seen it," Mrs. Lovelace broke in. "No one . . ."

"No one else has probably looked," Miss Pickerell retorted. "Or if they did, they couldn't put two and two together. It is my belief that this is the oil spill that the newspapers have just begun to mention and that you are stuffing those papers into the coal stove because you don't want your guests to know about it. You are afraid that most of them will not want to spend their holidays looking at the bodies of gulls and pelicans and terns and whatever else gets washed ashore in an oil spill."

Mrs. Lovelace opened her mouth to speak. Miss Pickerell ignored her.

"It is also my opinion," she went on, "that you should be encouraging your guests, instead, to clean up the beach and to rescue the birds and to help bathe the oil off such poor creatures as the tern and the sandpipers that are, at this very moment, out on your lawn. As a matter of fact, I may even start organizing the guests in this rescue operation myself."

Mr. Lovelace laughed again, this time while he signaled for his wife to remain silent.

"You have a suspicious nature, Miss Pickerell," he said. "I can assure you that everything is under control."

"You mean the hole has been repaired?" Miss Pickerell demanded.

"Yes," Mr. Lovelace said, nodding.

"And you know that the hole is no longer leaking?" Miss Pickerell questioned.

"Yes," Mr. Lovelace repeated.

"And the beach has also been cleared up?" she asked.

"Yes," Mr. Lovelace said again.

"And the poor birds are being helped?" she continued.

"Of course," said Mr. Lovelace.

Miss Pickerell looked back for another glance through the window at the tern and the sandpipers. She did not believe a word Mr. Lovelace said.

"I will go and see for myself," she told him.

Mr. Lovelace drew himself up to his very gaunt height. His eyes blazed with a cold intense fury. But he moved aside to let her pass. Miss Pickerell marched silently through the door.

"No!" Mrs. Lovelace called frantically after her. "There are icy patches near the water. You will fall, Miss Pickerell. You . . ."

"I have my umbrella to lean on," Miss Pickerell called back. "And I always wear sensible shoes."

"I will go with her," Mr. Lovelace said to his wife, and then added to Miss Pickerell, as he quickly stepped alongside of her, "to make sure that you do not fall, Miss Pickerell. To make *absolutely* sure!"

8

ENCOUNTER WITH
MR. LOVELACE

Mr. Lovelace did not say a word as they walked to the entrance hall. But he shook his head when Miss Pickerell started to go out the front way. He led her to the right of the desk where a swinging door opened onto a narrow corridor. The clatter of pans through one of the corridor walls seemed to indicate that they were in the vicinity of the kitchen. Miss Pickerell asked no questions. She followed Mr. Lovelace silently, as he made a sharp turn and then marched along a short passageway that ended in a tiny lobby.

"A side entrance to the house," she thought to herself.

She noticed the scrubbed look of the linoleum on the lobby floor and sniffed appreciatively at the smell of the brass polish on the doorknob. Whatever else Mrs.

Lovelace could or could not do, Miss Pickerell reflected, she certainly knew how to keep a house.

The wild screeching of a gull reached her ears the minute she and Mr. Lovelace stepped outside. It was a ring-billed gull, she observed, with greenish legs and a black ring encircling the yellow beak. She was able to see the colors so clearly because the gull lay sprawled at the edge of the lawn they were passing.

"Oil drove him away from the beach," Miss Pickerell said bitterly. "He's trying so hard now to live."

"Your imagination is simply extraordinary, Miss Pickerell," Mr. Lovelace commented. "I have never known one quite like it."

"May I remind you, Mr. Lovelace, that I am not blind," Miss Pickerell retorted swiftly. "On the contrary, my vision is a perfect 20/20. In both eyes. With my glasses on, that is."

Mr. Lovelace made no reply.

They crossed the gravel drive that bordered the lawn and began the descent on the path leading to the ocean. It was not really very steep, Miss Pickerell saw, and

ordinarily she would not have given it another thought. But the ice she met every
few feet kept slowing her down. And once,
when she saw a mother horseshoe crab
dragging herself and the three babies she
carried on her back away from the oily
water, she stopped altogether.

"I know you can't live unless you're in salt
water," she said, bending down to talk to the
mother crab. "And I can't take you back to

the ocean until it's cleaned up. But I'll find a way to help you. You and your poor babies! I promise!!"

She took a firm grip of her umbrella and proceeded down the path. Mr. Lovelace was no longer in sight ahead of her. She had no idea where he'd gone.

"It doesn't matter," she said. "I'll just go on without him."

She continued along the path, pausing only when she found herself facing a sharp incline that rose unexpectedly in front of her. Panting a little and leaning on her umbrella, she hastened up the incline.

"Forevermore!" she whispered when she reached the top.

Directly below her lay the ocean, its surf roaring and its small swells making gentle, lapping sounds. And there stuck on the shoals and keeled over where it had floundered, stood the enormous ship.

"Forevermore!" Miss Pickerell said again, this time while she polished her glasses with the handkerchief she took out of her bag and took another look.

She could see the oil clearly now. It was bubbling up from somewhere and it was fanning out in an ever-widening circle. What's more, the ocean currents were carrying it on the incoming tide closer and closer to the shore. She could hardly bear to watch. She turned away, sighing.

It was when she was refolding her handkerchief to put it back in her knitting bag that she heard the stealthy footsteps behind her. She wheeled around instantly. Mr. Lovelace, a long-handled shovel cradled in both arms, was moving up beside her.

"Did I surprise you, Miss Pickerell?" he asked, his eyes hard and his voice hoarse and low. "I didn't mean to do that. I meant for you *not* to hear me, actually."

Miss Pickerell did not answer. She suddenly remembered why Mr. Lovelace had seemed familiar to her when she first saw him in the dining room. He was the man with the dead birds, the man who had disappeared among the pine trees when Mrs. Lovelace was driving her from the station to the Lodge. He was carrying a shovel then, too. He probably used it to bury the dead birds he didn't want the guests to see. At this moment, he was unfolding his arms and raising the shovel above his head.

"No!" Miss Pickerell screamed.

She leaned back to get out of the way of the blow she expected. She paid no attention to the sand that began to slide away under her feet.

"No," Mr. Lovelace said softly. "I am not going to bash your head in with the shovel, Miss Pickerell. I am not going to push you down the slope, either. But, as my wife tried to warn you, you may very well fall down all by yourself."

He made no move to stop her when she lost her balance. Her umbrella and her knitting bag dangling, she tumbled, head over heels, down to the beach below. She landed, nearly unconscious, on a pair of enormous wading boots.

The boots moved. A voice above them said gruffly, "No unauthorized personnel allowed here, Miss! No trespassing of any kind! I'm the watchman assigned to guard the tanker."

Miss Pickerell struggled to rouse herself. She shook her head as hard as she could from side to side. Then she took several deep breaths and got up on her feet. After a few more deep breaths, she brushed the sand off her clothes, resettled the glasses which had slipped halfway down her nose, and looked contemptuously at the man with the thick white sideburns and very red cheeks standing in front of her.

"I haven't come here to spy on your tanker," she told him. "I want to do something about that oil spill."

"That's as may be," the man replied. "I'm not saying I don't believe you. But nothing gets done overnight. These things take time."

"Much too much time for the dying birds and the helpless sea creatures," Miss Pickerell answered briskly.

She turned her back on the watchman and, lost in thought, walked very slowly up the sandy hill toward the Three Chimney Lodge.

9

MISS PICKERELL MAKES UP HER MIND

"I'll *have* to call the Governor," she kept repeating to herself, as she walked into the little lobby and, from there, back through the entrance hall to the front door. "I'll have to get him to do *something* about this oil spill. I don't care if it *is* Sunday and his day off."

The sound of Mrs. Lovelace calling outside for her husband and the squeak of a door from somewhere inside hastened her footsteps.

"I can use the telephone in a neighbor's house," she told herself, practically. "Or I can hail a bus or taxi to take me to the nearest public telephone."

But there was no neighbor's house anywhere, she saw, when she walked between the two elm trees. And the only thing moving on the road was a snow plough, zigzagging slowly along leaving a trail of sand. Miss Pickerell stepped into the middle of the road immediately and waved with her umbrella.

"You-hoo!" she shouted. "You-hoo!"

The snow plough came to a halt. A man wearing a green and white helmet strapped tightly under his chin looked down at her inquiringly.

"Emergency!" Miss Pickerell called up to him. "To the nearest public telephone, please!"

The man opened the cab door and motioned for her to climb in.

"I'm new here," he said. "So far, I haven't seen any public telephones. Maybe in Wickam, the next town up. Or in Chickam, going the other way."

"Chickam," Miss Pickerell replied instantly, remembering the two antique shops that Mrs. Lovelace had mentioned. "Please take me there."

Ten minutes later, she stood in front of a shop with two dusty gas lamps, a sack full of colored glass marbles, and an old school clock in the window. A sign with the words MRS. MIRANDA PRISM, ANTIQUES, printed on it in red letters, hung above a large brass

knocker. Miss Pickerell gave the knocker a
hard tap. A buzzer released the door.

At first glance, the inside of MRS. MIRANDA
PRISM, ANTIQUES looked like an old-
fashioned general store. Bolts of cloth and
spools of silk and cotton thread lined the

shelves to the right. The shelves to the left held trays of home-baked bread and a tall stack of milk pails. Miss Pickerell walked quickly past these, then around two tables piled high with patchwork quilts, and on up to the rear of the shop where someone seemed to be moving behind a hand-painted screen that had one broken leg. Miss Pickerell was sure that this was a genuine antique.

"Hello!" she called impatiently. "If . . . if you don't mind, I'd like to talk to you."

A woman with yellow hair, arranged almost as elaborately as Mrs. Broadribb's, and with bracelets hanging from each wrist pushed the screen aside.

"I'm inclined to catch cold easily," she apologized. "Especially in the ears. And when that door keeps opening . . ."

Miss Pickerell thought she might tell Mrs. Prism afterward about how soothing warm camphorated oil could be for a cold in the ears. At the moment, however, she had more important things to do.

"I'd like to use your telephone," she said. "Please! It's an emergency!"

Mrs. Prism nodded understandingly. She led Miss Pickerell to a small back room where a telephone stood on a half-open carton of paperback books. Miss Pickerell dialed the Governor's number immediately. The Governor's wife answered on the very first ring.

"I have the flu," she announced to Miss Pickerell. "I was just on the way to the kitchen to get some hot tea. I must have caught the germs from the Governor. He had it before me. He's still not over it."

She absolutely refused to disturb the Governor who, she said, had fallen asleep only five minutes ago. Nothing that Miss Pickerell told her about the importance of the call could change her mind.

"The Governor needs his rest," she insisted, and hung up with a bang.

Miss Pickerell took her little address book out of her knitting bag, looked up the number of her friend Clara Swiftlee, the lady assistant sheriff, and dialed again. This time, the telephone rang several times before anyone picked up the receiver. Miss Pickerell recalled that she had never thought the assistant sheriff's new secretary was very efficient.

"No," the girl told her, "Assistant Sheriff Swiftlee is not here. She's out on a shoplifting case. No, the sheriff is not in his office, either. I don't know exactly where he . . ."

"I know," the unmistakably nasal voice of Miss Lemmon, Square Toe City's telephone operator, broke in. "He's chasing the man who picked up the two litter baskets on the corner of Hickory Lane and . . . Oh, dear, I didn't mean to listen in. Oh . . ."

Her voice faded out with a nervous laugh. The secretary was no longer on the line, either. Miss Pickerell held the silent receiver to her ear while she considered whom else she might call.

"There's Professor Humwhistel," she decided. "And Dr. Haggerty. And even Mr. Clanghorn, at the *Square Toe Gazette.* One of *them* will know what to do.

But Miss Lemmon's voice, coming on the line again, very officially told her that Professor Humwhistel's telephone was temporarily out of order. Dr. Haggerty's nurse advised her that he was in the operating room with a puppy who had broken his left front paw. And Mr. Clanghorn's line was busy. Miss Pickerell gave up.

"It's probably just as well," she murmured. "I know *exactly* what I have to do. I've known all along, really. I just wanted to talk to someone because I didn't want to face it."

She asked the local operator how much she owed for her calls, counted out the change, and chose two paperback books to bring back to Euphus and Rosemary. There were some extremely long words in the books, she noticed. But she was sure that Euphus and Rosemary would understand them. They were both very good readers.

Mrs. Prism was busy putting a china doll into the window when Miss Pickerell walked back into the shop. The doll had on a starched white dress with a pink ribbon threaded through the lace at the neck and around the waist.

"I had a doll like that once," Miss Pickerell said.

"I did, too," Mrs. Prism sighed. "Those were the days!"

She wrapped up Miss Pickerell's books for her and told her where to find a taxi. The taxi stand was one block down, directly across from the railroad depot. Miss Pickerell saw the train belching smoke and pulling out of the station just as she approached. She thought she also saw Mortimor Tooting's freckled face peering out through one of the windows while she was telling the taxi driver where to take her.

"I suppose I should have listened to young Mortimor," she muttered, as she settled back against the plastic seat covers. "I suppose I should have listened and gone straight back to my nice, quiet farm. I'm too tired for any more outlandish adventures."

"Did you say something?" the taxi driver asked.

"Yes," said Miss Pickerell. "I am about to go down into the ocean to plug up a hole in a supertanker."

The taxi driver stared.

10

INTO THE HOLD OF
THE SUPERTANKER

Miss Pickerell hesitated for only an instant
after she took her scuba equipment out of
the closet. She changed hastily into her
tight-fitting rubber suit, strapped the oxygen tank across her back, put on her face
mask, and pulled on her rubber flippers.
Then she sat down on the bed to figure out
her plan of operation. It was one thing to
make a firm resolution. It was quite another
to carry it out. How was she going to fill up
the hole? And how was she going to get out
of the Lodge to do this, in the first place?

The matter of the hole, she decided, was
not too difficult. She was an excellent swim-
mer. She could easily manage to get down
to the hole. And she would close it up with
something she'd find on the beach.

"I'll look for something that will fit snug-
ly," she told herself. "For the time being, at

least. The Governor can send someone to do a more thorough job when he's recovered from his flu."

She made a mental note to remind him and thought about the problem of getting out of the house. With her scuba suit on, she could not hope to escape attention. The guests would surely ask questions, and as for Mr. Lovelace . . . she didn't know exactly what *he* would do. She had hardly dared look at him or at Mrs. Lovelace when she stopped at the desk for her key.

"There *must* be a way to get out unnoticed," she said, as she paced up and down the bedroom floor. "There *has* to be!"

A thousand memories of miraculous escapes she had seen in her favorite old movies popped into her head. One actor, she remembered, used to slide down a pipe to the ground and then jump over everything that stood in his way. Another was always leaping into the dumbwaiter that carried the dishes to and from the kitchen. Now, if she could only . . . With an effort, she shook off these wild flights of her imagination and walked over to the window.

Most of the guests, she saw, were basking in the sunshine on the front lawn. They lounged in canvas chairs, facing Mrs. Gladys Goodbody, who sat upright on a high stool. She was reading from a book she held before her. The Frowley sisters were not listening. They sat at a table, playing Scrabble. Mr. and Mrs. Slitherspoon were not listening, either. They were arguing about how to get a big package out of the rear of the Lovelace station wagon. The package would not budge, no matter how hard Mrs. Slitherspoon pushed it from inside the car and Mr. Slitherspoon pulled it from the outside.

"One thing is certain," Miss Pickerell said, as she turned away from the window. "I can't go out the front way because Mr. and Mrs. Lovelace are there. And I can't go out the back way with everybody on the lawn. I'm not even sure I can get to the side door with Mr. and Mrs. Lovelace right there at the desk."

She stopped pacing when she remembered the door with the squeak, the one she heard when Mrs. Lovelace was calling for her husband and . . .

"That's still another door!" Miss Pickerell reasoned. "And it must be somewhere!!"

She peered cautiously out into the corridor. On her left were four neatly numbered guest rooms leading up to a blank wall. On her right were more guest rooms ending at . . .

"Mercy!" she exclaimed when she saw the iron door with the signaling red lights above it and the words FIRE EXIT clearly printed on the side.

She padded toward the door and jiggled the rusty bolt that held it tight. She was thinking that this was unquestionably a fire violation when she jerked it loose and stumbled down the stairs.

"Oh!" she cried the moment she stepped outside.

She had landed at the far left of the Three Chimney Lodge, around the corner from the back lawn and just across the drive from the old barn. She considered her position carefully.

"Yes," she concluded. "If I can walk around the barn and get on the path *that* way, no one will notice me and I'll manage."

But her flippers made loud crunching sounds when she hopped across the gravel. And the ice patches crackled underfoot as she dodged behind the barn and onto the path. She did not actually breathe freely

until she had climbed up to the rocky ledge
and down again on the other side to the
beach. The watchman, she noted happily,
seemed to be nowhere around. She hoped
he'd gone somewhere for coffee and that he
would take his time about drinking it.

The tide was high and the tanker was not
as close to the shore as she had expected.

She was able to catch glimpses of the jagged
hole only with the rise and fall of the
incoming waves. It was right near the front
and, she thought, about eighty feet down
from the deck. She measured the hole with
her eyes and quickly began to search for a
suitable plug. She picked up and discarded
four plastic detergent containers, each one
a different size and shape, two cork buoy
markers, and a worn-out life preserver.

"Maybe I ought to go search near the dunes," she told herself, briskly waddling off in that direction.

The sharp object that her left flipper bumped into on her third step nearly made her cry out in pain. She looked down to see a half-buried kickboard. The words THIS BELONGS TO JENNIFER were printed in large red letters across the top. Miss Pickerell stared. She could hardly believe her good fortune.

"Thank you, Jennifer, wherever you are," she whispered. "You've given me exactly what I need."

In less than a minute, she had pulled the board free of the sand, turned on the air in her scuba tank, put the connecting rubber hose into her mouth, and was swimming toward the tanker. Holding the board straight out ahead of her, she kicked hard and fast with her flippers. She tried not to think about all the dead sea creatures that she pushed aside as she headed for the hole. The waves kept covering it when they rose. But Miss Pickerell waited, treading water patiently, right in front of the hole. The minute a passing wave made it completely visible, she shoved the board in place. It popped out immediately.

"Oh, no!" Miss Pickerell groaned into her mouthpiece.

She wracked her brains, trying to figure out what was wrong with her solution. Idea after idea raced through her head, but not one brought her any closer to the answer.

"I'm too tired to think clearly," she told herself crossly. "And I *must!*"

But only aimless thoughts kept drifting

into her mind. She thought about Euphus and Professor Humwhistel at her surprise Valentine's Day party, about Mortimor Tooting on the train ride, about Mr. Slitherspoon's unusual variety salad, about his argument with his wife over the bulky package in the . . . She came to with a start. She felt distinctly annoyed with herself.

"I suppose I'm even more tired than I realized," she sighed. "Or I'd have known what to do the minute I watched Mr. and Mrs. Slitherspoon. I need to plug the hole from the *inside* so that the pressure of the oil against the board will make it stick fast. *That's* what was happening to their package. The pressure was holding it fast—"

She swam around the ship to look for a way to get up on deck. She stopped short when she saw a steel ladder bolted on the far side of the tanker. Miss Pickerell hated ladders. They made her dizzy.

"Well," she told herself consolingly, "at least it's on the far side where that watchman can't see me. He's probably finished his coffee by now."

She closed her eyes and began climbing up, rung by rung. She opened them again when her hands felt that they had reached

the top. She crossed the deck without further hesitation, located the storage tank with the leak, and, after a murmured "Forevermore," plunged down into the depths.

The oil enveloped her immediately. She could not even see until she had groped her way to where the light shone into the hole. The very next moment, she had the kickboard wedged where she wanted it. To make absolutely sure that it was jammed tight, she pushed against it with her shoulder.

Bubbles burst out in an instant explosion. The air hissed out of the tank instead of into the hose. Oil gushed into Miss Pickerell's mouth. And her groping fingers felt the long rip that was spreading across one side of the air hose and the split that gaped along the right shoulder of her wet suit.

"It must have torn when I pushed against the board," she gasped.

She was choking for want of air. With every ounce of energy she had left, she kicked herself up to the surface and began treading water frantically.

"I mustn't panic! I mustn't panic!" she kept telling herself.

But she knew that her strength was giving out. She realized that she could not go on kicking and treading water for much longer. And once she stopped, she would definitely drown!

11

IN THE NICK OF TIME

The arm that grasped her around the waist had a voice connected to it somewhere. The sound came from far away and reached her ears only as a faint, indistinct murmur. There were also strong arms that were pulling her up and carrying her down the long ladder and into the ocean. And then someone was holding her in a life-saver's grip, swimming back to shore with her, and placing her gently on the sand, while hands removed her mask and oxygen tank and fingers cleaned the oil from her face. Miss Pickerell opened her eyes and saw Mortimor Tooting.

"How . . . how . . . ?" she began.

She could not go on. She lay on the sand where he had settled her and she tried to find her breath. At the end of five minutes, she sat up.

"What are *you* doing here?" she asked.

"Just visiting," Mortimor Tooting said, grinning.

Miss Pickerell gazed at him blankly. Her mind was still not very clear, but she tried to force the haze away and to pull herself back to full consciousness.

"I . . . I mean," she asked, "how did you know I was in trouble?"

"I guessed," Mortimor replied. "When I saw you through the train window at Chickam, I thought something must be happening. I got off at Wickam, the next station, and took the train going back to Chickam."

"But . . . but your job?" Miss Pickerell asked.

"I telephoned Mr. Esticott from Wickam," Mortimor explained. "He thought I was absolutely right. He said he would take my place at the snack bar for as long as is necessary."

Miss Pickerell smiled.

"You saved my life, you know," she said gently. "You . . . you came in the nick of time."

Mortimor blushed through all his freckles.

"It was nothing," he said, grinning again.

Miss Pickerell went on with her questioning.

"I still don't understand," she said. "Who told you I went down to the ocean front?"

"A little man with a beard," Mortimor said promptly.

"Mr. Slitherspoon!" Miss Pickerell whispered.

"He didn't tell me exactly," Mortimor Tooting went on. "But when everybody on the lawn said they had no idea where you were, he called me over. Then he took me into the barn and suggested that I borrow his scuba equipment. He keeps it there, together with a lot of other . . ."

"He saw me!" Miss Pickerell interrupted. "He saw me and didn't say anything! He knew about the oil spill!!"

"Maybe," Mortimor commented. "Or maybe he just thought you liked scuba diving."

"But," Miss Pickerell insisted,"but then how did you know about the oil tanker?"

"That part was easy," Mortimor replied. "I remembered how upset you were about oil slicks when we talked on the train. And when I saw that supertanker surrounded by all that oily water, I knew. I just knew where you were."

"Oh!" Miss Pickerell said, thinking to herself that young Mortimor Tooting might very well be even smarter than Euphus. She planned to introduce him to her middle nephew the first chance she had.

"You are a real heroine, Miss Pickerell," Mortimor went on admiringly. "You plugged up that hole all by yourself."

Miss Pickerell shook her head sadly.

"Plugging up the hole was only the first step," she said. "Now, we have to do something about getting rid of the oil."

"I'll report it to the authorities," Mortimor Tooting promised. "They'll send someone."

Miss Pickerell shook her head again.

"It has been reported," she sighed. "The only one they've sent is a watchman."

"Oh?" asked Mortimor.

"And that watchman was absolutely right when he told me that these things take time," she added bitterly. She recalled only too well the time she had reported a broken traffic light on Mulberry Avenue, right off Main Street, in Square Toe City. No one came to fix it for nearly a week. The gulls and the terns and the sandpipers and the poor mother horseshoe crab with her babies couldn't wait that long.

She made a resolute effort to get up on her feet and stumbled as she did so.

"You need to rest," Mortimor Tooting suggested.

"Not at all," Miss Pickerell told him shakily. "I need to *think!*"

Very slowly and holding on to Mortimor's

strong right arm, she pulled herself upright and looked in the direction of the Three Chimney Lodge.

"We have a lot to talk about, Mortimor," she said. "Where is your microbiology book?"

"My microbiology book?" Mortimor repeated.

"Yes," Miss Pickerell said firmly, though she had not the faintest hope that she could begin to understand even half of the scientific words in it. "Where is the microbiology book you were reading on the train?"

"In the barn," Mortimor Tooting told her. "In the barn where my clothes are."

"I'll meet you there," Miss Pickerell said briskly. "As soon as I get out of my wet bathing suit."

"Scuba suit," Mortimor corrected.

"Thank you," Miss Pickerell replied.

She felt better already now that she had made up her mind about what to do next. She paid no attention to the watchman who was now calling to her from the side of one of the dunes. She began, for the third time, to walk up the sandy hill.

At the top, she paused for a second to glance at the back lawn. Mrs. Goodbody was still sitting on her stool, reading from her book. The Frowley sisters had stopped playing Scrabble and were dozing in their chairs. Mr. Jeetowitz, Junior, had joined the Slitherspoons who were still arguing near the station wagon. Mr. and Mrs. Lovelace were nowhere in sight. Miss Pickerell smiled and crossed to the gravel driveway.

She left Mortimor Tooting at the barn. While he stood guard, she ran around the barn and proceeded to the side entrance. She raced up the stairs, two at a time, resolutely pushed open the fire door, and sped along the corridor to her room. In three minutes, her umbrella and her knitting bag on her arm and her sweater over her shoulders, she was out again and on her way to join Mortimor Tooting in the barn.

12

MISS PICKERELL HAS AN IDEA

Mr. Lovelace's barn was not at all what Miss Pickerell had expected. It had no place for cows to be milked, no hay loft, not even any old tools. Actually, it looked more like an attic. A sewing machine and a dressmaker's dummy with a half-finished pink blouse draped over it stood on the right side, next to a broken-down phonograph and two unpainted kitchen chairs. The left side was filled with packing cases, each one neatly labeled YEAST TABLETS. The last packing case leaned against a brown wooden icebox. A shelf holding upside-down glass jars full of fruit and vegetable preserves was attached to the wall above the icebox.

"I'm glad to see that Mrs. Lovelace is as careful about her preserves as she is about the rest of her housekeeping," Miss Pickerell commented approvingly.

"I beg your pardon?" Mortimor Tooting asked.

"She's made sure to put her jars upside down," Miss Pickerell explained, "so that she can tell at a glance whether . . ."

Mortimor Tooting was not listening. He was examining the inside of the icebox.

"I could use a glass of milk," he said.

But there was no milk in the icebox. There was only Mr. Slitherspoon's squash, lying on top of his onions, cucumbers, beets, and parsnips. Miss Pickerell, looking too, observed that a large bunch of purple grapes lay in the corner. She was thinking that she might suggest some of these to Mortimor Tooting as a substitute for the milk, when she noticed the mildew on them. She quickly closed the icebox door and turned to her young friend.

"As I told you before, Mortimor," she said, "we have to *think.*"

"Yes," Mortimor replied, pulling a chair up for her and helping her to settle her knitting bag and her umbrella on the packing case that leaned against the icebox. "Where do we begin?"

"With what you explained to me on the train in regard to the oil-eating process,"

Miss Pickerell answered promptly. "Now, in the notes that Euphus made, he . . ."

She interrupted herself to consult the piece of paper that she took out of her knitting bag. Mortimor pulled the second kitchen chair up next to her and scrutinized the notes with her.

"I wish your nephew had a better handwriting," he commented.

Miss Pickerell nodded her agreement while she pointed to the first words she was able to make out.

"Oil-eating microbes," she read, and added, "You did say, didn't you, Mortimor, that these microbes sometimes refuse to eat up all the oil?"

"I certainly did," Mortimor replied.

"And these hydrocarbons that Euphus mentions," Miss Pickerell went on, pointing to another word on his list. "They are what oil is made up of. We talked about that on the train."

"Yes," Mortimor said. "Some of those hydrocarbons are the things the microbes can't break down."

"But," Miss Pickerell stated quickly, "the new microbes you told me about eat *everything* up."

"Well," Mortimor said hesitantly, "that's what they're supposed to do. It's all in the experimental stage in the laboratory and . . ."

"Then, as I believe I commented before," Miss Pickerell interrupted, "it's about time the experiment got out of the laboratory. How do we go about breeding these microbes?"

"*We?*" Mortimor Tooting asked, staring.

"We," Miss Pickerell repeated. "Please tell me all you know."

The young man opened and closed his microbiology book.

"I'm sure that information is not in here," he said. "But I remember what our science professor told us. He called the new microbes a superstrain. And he explained that this superstrain can even go on to convert the hydrocarbons into a protein and that the protein can then be a good food for the marine life and . . ."

"Nevermind that for the moment," Miss Pickerell interrupted again. "What we have to do now is *start*."

Mortimor Tooting swallowed hard.

"How?" he asked.

Miss Pickerell answered by putting Euphus's list back in her knitting bag and taking her ball-point pen and an old laundry list out of it.

"I always think better with a pen or a pencil in my hand," she said, as she turned the laundry list over and wrote on the back of it the word FUNGI and, under that, the word BACTERIA.

Mortimor Tooting leaned forward to read what she was writing.

"Right!" he exclaimed. "Fungi and bacteria are definitely components of the superstrain my professor was describing."

"Well, we have plenty of fungi around," Miss Pickerell replied quickly. "There are some mildewed grapes in the right-hand corner of the icebox. Please bring them here."

"Mildewed grapes!" Mortimor shouted. "I *know* that the downy mildew found on grapes contains oomycetes, a form of aquatic fungi. But . . . but how did *you* know, Miss Pickerell?"

"Everybody knows that molds, mildews, and rusts have fungi," Miss Pickerell replied, while she put an equal sign next to the word FUNGI on the back of her laundry list and added the words MILDEWED GRAPES.

"But, *aquatic fungi*," Mortimor insisted, as he ran to get the grapes. "How did you know *that* about mildew?"

"I didn't, exactly," Miss Pickerell said, as she thought hard about what to use for bacteria. Nothing occurred to her. She began to pace up and down in the barn, hoping that the exercise would help her brain work better. Then she crossed to the shelf with the upside-down jars.

"I've been putting up preserves like these for almost as long as I can remember," she said, thoughtfully, as she picked up one jar after another and searched under the lids. "Now, this jar of beans . . . yes, just as I thought. Here's the telltale stain. That means, Mortimor, Mrs. Loveace has one spoiled jar. And . . ."

"And?" Mortimor asked.

"And we have our bacteria!" Miss Pickerell concluded triumphantly.

Mortimor shook his head sadly.

"Spoiled beans are no good, Miss Pickerell, he said." They have the wrong kind of bacteria. We need the kind that's found in aquatic life. Bacteria like that are called Pseudomonas and can be found in oysters, scallops, shellfish . . ."

"Stop! Stop!" Miss Pickerell shouted. "Another spoiled jar! And *these* are pickled clams . . .!"

"They don't *have* to be spoiled!" Mortimor exclaimed, also shouting. "All clams have the bacteria we need."

"Better to be sure," Miss Pickerell told him, rushing back with the spoiled jar and picking up the laundry list.

Mortimor watched intently while she rapidly wrote next to the word BACTERIA and after the equal sign, the words SPOILED CLAMS.

"And now," Miss Pickerell said, when she finished, "I'm ready, if you are!"

Mortimor Tooting sat down. He opened his mouth, shut it, then opened it again.

"I'm sorry, Miss Pickerell," he said. "I just thought of another thing my professor said. He said it was necessary to include something to decompose the oil, but . . ."

"Yes?" Miss Pickerell asked.

Mortimor did not look at her when he answered.

"But," he went on, "he didn't tell us just what it was. Or, if he did, I don't remember . . ."

"You will," Miss Pickerell said encouragingly. "In a little while. That is, if he really did mention it."

They both sat, waiting. Mortimor hung his head. Miss Pickerell stared at the cases labeled YEAST TABLETS. Something about those words kept nagging at her. It reminded her of an event that had to do with oil. But no matter how she tried, she couldn't recall what it was.

"My cat, Pumpkins," she said absently, "loves yeast. It's good for him. My veterinarian told me to give him at least one tablet a day. I always keep a bottle in the house."

"Oh?" Mortimor asked.

"Yes," Miss Pickerell replied. "Sometimes, he turns up his nose when I give him the tablet. That's very unusual, though."

"Oh!" Mortimor said again.

"And sometimes," Miss Pickerell continued, "he insists on having one tablet after another. Once, when the bottle was open, he turned it over and ate all the tablets that had fallen into the sink. I was very busy that day, trying to oil a creaky hinge on my kitchen door. The oil I was using spilled on the floor, and . . ."

She stopped suddenly. She knew now what Mr. Slitherspoon's yeast reminded her of. It was what Mr. Kettelson had explained to her.

"My hardware store man told me to use yeast to soak up hard-to-remove stains," she burst out. "The principle is the same. We . . . we . . ."

She leaped out of her chair and began pulling bottles out of the boxes in the packing case. Mortimor bent immediately over his microbiology book.

"Here, Miss Pickerell!" he shouted. "Here's a picture of kerosine globules being decomposed by the yeast cells that were coated on them."

"And yeast can decompose the oil from the tanker the same way!" Miss Pickerell added, as she picked up her laundry list to mark this down. She read everything out loud rapidly to Mortimor Tooting:

"That's it," she declared.

Mortimor looked at her hesitantly.

"I don't know, Miss Pickerell," he said. "Scientists use what they call genetic engineering to construct what they call a superstrain. It takes a very long time and . . ."

"We don't have a very long time," Miss Pickerell interrupted to tell him.

"And," Mortimor went on, "it's all planned very scientifically. I'm not sure that just throwing a lot of different organisms together is going to work."

"Is there any harm in trying?" Miss Pickerell asked sharply.

"No," Mortimor admitted. "And I do remember about the yeast now. My professor did mention it. He also mentioned sodium chloride to activate the yeast genes when they are mixed into . . ."

"Sodium chloride!" Miss Pickerell laughed. "I know what that is. I looked it up in my encyclopedia once. The S volume. Those two long words mean just plain salt. Run back to the Lodge and get some, Mortimor! Run fast!!"

13

A WILD EXPERIMENT

Miss Pickerell did not even take the trouble to cast a backward glance at the Three Chimney Lodge as she scrambled down the hill. There was *no* way Mr. Lovelace could persuade her to give up the experiment, she thought to herself. And if, by any chance, he tried to stop her *forcibly,* young Mortimor Tooting was right there by her side for protection. He had brought two salt shakers with him from the coffee lounge and a box of aluminum foil that, he said, he had picked up in the deserted kitchen. The grapes, clams, and yeast were wrapped up in some of the aluminum foil. Mortimor carried this in his arms. Miss Pickerell held onto the salt shakers and the rest of the aluminum foil with one hand and to her umbrella and knitting bag with the other.

"We'll have to find an oil-soaked piece of

ground on which to work," Mortimor said as they neared the ocean front. "A small patch that's not frozen. Decomposition depends a lot on water temperature. If the water from the melting ice in the patch is approximately 25°C, we'll have a pretty fast degrading of the oil."

Miss Pickerell tried mentally to translate 25°C into Fahrenheit degrees. She thought that 77°F. might be about right. The temperature of the air around her certainly felt way up. She could only *hope* that the temperature of the water was what they needed.

Mortimor was using his feet to test the oily patches of ground that he saw. Miss Pickerell poked around with the tip of her umbrella. She moved step by step away from the ocean. The sand seemed to her to be softer here. She poked with special care when she found a heavily oiled patch about six inches in diameter that appeared to have particularly loose sand. Mortimor agreed that this patch might be good for the experiment when she showed it to him.

"We have to mash up the yeast and then add the grapes and the clams and pour on some salt," he said. "We have to mix every-thing up into a kind of mush."

"The grapes are already falling apart," Miss Pickerell said, glancing at them while she spread a fresh sheet of aluminum foil on a flat piece of wood Mortimor placed between them.

Mortimor poured the pickled clams out onto the aluminum foil.

"I guess you'll want to work on the yeast tablets," he said to her. "You'll probably do them very fast because of your practice with Pumpkins."

"Pumpkins crushes his own," Miss Pickerell informed him. "With his teeth."

Mortimor made no comment. He was busy shaking the salt over the grapes and clams and over the ground yeast that Miss Pickerell was rapidly adding to the pile.

"And now," Mortimor said, "we need some sort of abrasive. Something that will release the genes from the cells without damaging them."

"What about more salt?" Miss Pickerell questioned.

"Salt's okay for the yeast," said Mortimor, "but we need an abrasive, not a stimulant for

these other cells. We can use sand, maybe."
He scooped up a handful and sprinkled it
over the rest of the ingredients. And then,
he got down on his knees and began gently
to knead it all together.

"We could also use something to moisten
everything," he added.

"Sea water," said Miss Pickerell, taking off
her hat and rushing to scoop up some water
that didn't look too oily.

While she poured, Mortimor mixed and

mixed and mixed. At last, he stopped and studied the pile of strange-looking mush between them.

"And now," he said, "I guess we can coat the globules on top of the patch."

He took a fistful of the mush and proceeded to spread it carefully and evenly over the globules of oil. Then he stood up and dusted the sand off his pants.

"It's a very wild experiment," he remarked. "My professor would not approve of any of it."

"No?" Miss Pickerell asked, getting up, too.

"No," Mortimor Tooting replied. "He'd talk about measurements and proportions and I don't know what else. He'd say that we didn't at all know what we were doing."

"I'm certain that Mr. Edison didn't *always* know *exactly* what *he* was doing when he invented the electric light," Miss Pickerell retorted. "He had an idea in his head and he tried and tried again."

"I suppose so," Mortimor admitted. "But Eli Whitney, who invented the . . ."

"And we," Miss Pickerell went on, firmly steering the conversation away from the inventors of history, "we have done what we think is right. What happens next, Mortimor?"

"Well," Mortimor said, a little uncertainly, "the bacteria and fungi should start decomposing the oily layers. And then, I think, the components in the oil begin to combine into large droplets."

"Droplets of oil?" Miss Pickerell questioned anxiously.

"The droplets don't spread," Mortimor replied. "They just stay there. I'm not sure what we do after that."

Miss Pickerell needed to think about this for only a minute.

"We pick them up, of course," she said. "We'll use a shovel and pick them up and take them away."

Mortimor looked at her respectfully.

"It's only common sense," Miss Pickerell added. "But tell me, Mortimor, how long will we have to wait for the droplets to form? It's such a very small patch. Will two hours be enough?"

Mortimor did not answer immediately. He was staring at a dead and swollen sea gull, lying where the snow had melted away from another ice patch.

"*If* it works," he said slowly. "If the experiment works, Miss Pickerell."

Miss Pickerell followed his gaze and looked quickly away.

"It *must* work," she said, almost shouting. "It *simply must!*"

14

A GLOOMY LUNCH

The late Sunday afternoon lunch at the Three Chimney Lodge was nearly over when Miss Pickerell entered the dining room and slid into her place next to Mrs. Slitherspoon. No one seemed to notice her. No one paid any attention to Mortimor Tooting, who sat down in an empty chair near the rubber plant, either. Everyone was staring at Mr. Slitherspoon.

He stood at the head of the table, nervously tugging at his beard. His small, round face was red with excitement.

"I tell you," he said, his voice unnaturally high, "that two bottles of my yeast tablets are missing. Also an entire bunch of grapes. I counted everything carefully. Twice!"

The Frowley sisters giggled.

"I never did like grapes," Floretta said.

"I noticed that you ate every single one on

your plate when I served them yesterday," Mr. Slitherspoon retorted, instantly.

Floretta stopped giggling. Coretta and Loretta flushed.

"And since," Mr. Slitherspoon went on, glaring at Mr. Lovelace while he spoke, "no guests, except myself, are permitted to enter the barn, I demand an explanation from the management."

Miss Pickerell looked across the room to catch Mortimor's eye. Mortimor shook his head. Mr. Slitherspoon noticed this immediately.

"I consider the young man who went into the barn with me this morning completely innocent," he said. "He is not the type to commit such a crime."

Mr. Lovelace, his hair hanging over his glowering face and his dark eyes furious, marched up from the kitchen door to stand in front of Mr. Slitherspoon.

"Are you accusing *me* of stealing your yeast and your grapes?" he asked.

Mr. Slitherspoon moved back a few steps. He did not answer. No one else said anything, either. The silence in the room felt to Miss Pickerell like the calm before a thunderstorm. She looked again at Mortimor

Tooting. He glanced at his watch and shook his head vigorously.

"I think that you *are* accusing me, Mr. Slitherspoon," Mr. Lovelace went on icily, "since you made a point of saying that no guests other than yourself were allowed to enter the barn."

"It is possible," Mr. Slitherspoon conceded, "that one of the guests did go into the

barn without permission. I didn't say that a guest couldn't have gone in."

The silence seemed to Miss Pickerell to grow almost thick with suspicion. She watched the Frowley sisters lower their heads and peer from beneath their eyelashes at the men on the opposite side of the table. They, in turn, kept their eyes fixed steadily on their laps. Mr. Jeetowitz, Junior, coughed once, then gave Mr. Beadle, who sat next to him, a quick, hard stare. Miss Pickerell also noticed Mrs. Lovelace, who was standing in back of the rubber plant, watching her stealthily.

"She . . . she knows!" Miss Pickerell whispered to herself. "Or, at least, she has an idea that I . . ."

She held her breath while she waited for Mrs. Lovelace to make the accusation.

It was Mrs. Gladys Goodbody's voice that broke the silence, however. She laughed a little before she spoke.

"I have a suggestion to make," she chirped. "We need to relax until we learn who did this dreadful thing. I believe we should all go and sit in the parlor."

"What an excellent idea!" Mrs. Lovelace exclaimed, immediately. "We'll play charades."

The guests started filing out of the room. Miss Pickerell, walking beside Mortimor Tooting, looked appealingly up at him.

"Impossible!" he hissed, glancing at his watch again. "The experiment needs more time."

"But . . . but . . . ," Miss Pickerell began.

"There's no telling what Mr. Lovelace

might do to it," Mortimor warned her. "Remember that!"

Her mind in a turmoil, Miss Pickerell sat down on the parlor sofa, next to Mr. Slitherspoon. She couldn't resist saying something comforting to him.

"I really wouldn't worry about your yeast and your grapes," she commented. "The person who took them may very well return them."

"Humph!" Mr. Slitherspoon snorted.

"Or if that isn't possible," Miss Pickerell added, "the person will pay for everything. I'm certain that person . . ."

A chord from the piano across the parlor interrupted her assurances to Mr. Slitherspoon. Mrs. Goodbody, sitting at the piano, let the chord die away and began to talk.

"I told Mrs. Lovelace," she said, "that charades weren't exactly what I had in mind. I explained to her that the children in the choir had asked me to write a little operetta for them and, naturally, I obliged. It's based on nursery rhymes and quite amusing."

Mr. Beadle and Mr. Fiedler, standing in the doorway with Mr. Deacon, Mr. Heating, and Mr. Jeetowitz, Junior, asked to be excused. Mr. Beadle tapped his forehead to show that he had a headache. Mr. Fiedler said that he was suffering from the same ailment.

"Too much sun," he sighed, as he left.

Mrs. Goodbody waved gaily to both of them and turned back to the piano.

"The first part of the operetta," she announced, "is about Little Bo Peep, who, as you all know, lost her sheep and didn't know where to find them. In this operetta, she loses her sisters and brothers. She goes from country to country looking for them. Of course, she has to learn how to ask in the different languages of the countries and she makes some funny mistakes. It's very enjoyable, I think."

She struck another chord on the piano, commented that the operetta, because it had so many foreign words in it, was also educational, and began. Miss Pickerell did not listen to more than the first six lines. She was too busy watching Mr. Deacon, Mr. Heating, and Mr. Jeetowitz, Junior, who were quietly walking out of the parlor, one by one, at approximately five-minute intervals. Mr. Jeetowitz, Junior, was the last to leave. Miss Pickerell sighed.

She looked around the room and up at the clock that hung on the wall in back of the piano. It was nearly forty minutes since Mrs. Gladys Goodbody had started her musical composition. Mr. Slitherspoon, tired from all the excitement, had fallen asleep. Every once in a while, he made a throaty, snoring sound. Mrs. Slitherspoon, settled on the other side of the sofa, reached over each time to nudge him. The Frowley sisters sat smiling in their chairs. Mr. and Mrs. Lovelace and young Mr. Mortimor Tooting stood silently near the piano. They applauded very loudly when Mrs. Goodbody ended her Bo Peep part of the operetta and rose to take a little bow. The applause woke Mr. Slitherspoon up.

"No!" he shouted. "I won't have it! I refuse, I absolutely refuse to sit here quietly in the same room with a th . . . I . . . I can't even say the word!"

"Of course not," Mrs. Goodbody commented. "No gentleman would."

"But . . . ," Mr. Slitherspoon began again.

Mr. Lovelace, scowling grimly, stepped into the middle of the room.

"I have no idea who your thief is, Mr. Slitherspoon," he said. "Since I am the owner of the Lodge, however, I will take full responsibility and pay you for your loss. I will pay up to the amount of . . ."

Miss Pickerell could bear it no longer. She waved her umbrella in the air and screamed frantically, "Stop! Stop!"

Everybody stared. Miss Pickerell took one more look at the clock.

"I can explain the whole thing," she said. "I was going to, anyway, in a little while. But I see it will have to be now. I took your yeast and your mildewed grapes, Mr. Slither-spoon."

A chorus of gasps, starting with the Frowley sisters and ending with Mrs. Lovelace, ran through the room.

"I did it to coat a patch of oily soil," Miss Pickerell went on. "Mr. Lovelace will understand what I mean. It was an experiment to see if new microbes, bred from bacteria and fungi, will eat up the oil so that it won't spread and destroy anybody or anything anymore."

Mr. Lovelace leaped from the middle of the room to stand over her.

"Where? Where?" he asked. "Where did you do this?"

"At the ocean front," Miss Pickerell said.

"On the beach near the water, a little to the left of the ledge where you . . ."

Mr. Lovelace did not wait to hear the rest. He ran so fast, he seemed almost to be flying out of the door. Miss Pickerell, with Mortimor Tooting hard on her heels, raced after him.

15

"YOU'VE DONE IT, MISS PICKERELL!"

Mr. Lovelace was already stooping over the experimental patch when Miss Pickerell and Mortimor Tooting caught up with him. Mortimor moved up alongside of Mr. Lovelace. Miss Pickerell squeezed herself between them.

"Oh!" she gasped.

"Oh!" Mortimor said, a little more cautiously.

"It's happening!" Miss Pickerell exclaimed.

"It does look like a droplet," Mortimor agreed.

"And there will be more and more," Miss Pickerell told him.

Mr. Lovelace looked at Miss Pickerell, then at Mortimor Tooting, and back again at Miss Pickerell.

"Will somebody please explain this to me?" he asked.

"Certainly," Miss Pickerell replied. "Mortimor is a student of science. He will tell you all about it."

Mortimor, staring down at the patch, made no comment.

"There's another one," he shouted suddenly. "Another droplet! You've done it, Miss Pickerell! You have made science history!!"

Mr. Lovelace looked again at Miss Pickerell.

"Please," he pleaded. "Please!"

"Well," Miss Pickerell said, trying to think it all out. "I suppose everything really started at the surprise Valentine's Day party that the members of THE MISS PICKERELL FAN CLUB, SQUARE TOE MOUNTAIN BRANCH, gave me."

"I'm a member," Mortimor stated proudly. "Of the Vittelstone Village Branch. And Mr. Slitherspoon, when he took me to the barn this morning, said he was organizing a Chickam County Branch. His three grandchildren are very eager to join."

"I feel very bad about Mr. Slitherspoon and his yeast and grapes," Miss Pickerell sighed. "I meant to leave a note in the icebox so that he wouldn't worry. I'm afraid I forgot about it in all the excitement."

"Yeast and grapes," Mr. Lovelace replied vaguely.

"And Mrs. Lovelace's pickled clams," Miss Pickerell added. "It was a spoiled jar. I didn't think she'd mind."

Mr. Lovelace said that he was extremely confused.

"I had to use all those items," Miss Pickerell told him. "You see, Euphus, my middle nephew, wrote on his homework paper that I saw at the Valentine's Day party that microbes can eat oil. Euphus is very smart in science. But Mortimor, who knows all about microbiology, said that the new supermicrobes are better eaters than the real microbes. And he told me that bacteria and fungi are needed to breed the supermicrobes."

"There are others," Mortimor commented. "Other things besides bacteria and fungi, I mean. But I couldn't remember them."

"Yeast and grapes," Mr. Lovelace repeated again. "*And* spoiled clams."

"We needed the yeast to decompose the oil," Miss Pickerell explained. "The mildewed grapes were for the fungi. And the spoiled clams had the bacteria."

"Miss Pickerell thought of them," Mortimor Tooting burst out. "She thinks of *everything!*"

"I had to think of something," Miss Pickerell said. "I couldn't bear doing nothing when I saw all those suffering terns and sea gulls and that poor mother horseshoe crab with her babies. . . . Thank heavens, I'll soon be able to put them back in the ocean. And I'll give those birds on your lawn a good bath."

"We were very lucky that the hydrocarbons in the oily patch we worked on reacted to the culture of bacteria and fungi that we fed it," Mortimor said, thoughtfully."This may or may not be true of other places. All sorts of other mixed cultures are being developed and tested right now."

"And Mortimor is studying very hard to learn all about them," Miss Pickerell said quickly.

Mr. Lovelace smiled.

"If you need a quiet place for your studies, Mr. Tooting," he said, "the Three Chimney Lodge is yours, free of charge, at any time. For experiments too, if you wish."

"Just wait till my professor hears about this!!" Mortimor shouted.

"And you, Miss Pickerell," Mr. Lovelace said, turning to her, "I owe you more than an apology."

"An apology will be enough," Miss Pickerell replied curtly.

"You have saved the Three Chimney Lodge," Mr. Lovelace went on.

"Only one patch," Miss Pickerell reminded him. "As Mortimor has mentioned, our culture may not work in all the other places. The Governor will have to send a scientific expedition to study the problem. I'll make *sure* that he does!"

"In either case," Mr. Lovelace said, sighing a little, "things will be somewhat easier for me from now on. It's a pity, Miss Pickerell, that life can't be as simple as it used to be."

Miss Pickerell looked at him thoughtfully.

"This morning, when I was in MRS. MIRANDA PRISM, ANTIQUES, I felt very tempted to buy a doll that I saw."

"For Rosemary!" Mortimor exclaimed. "Mr. Esticott has told me all about Rosemary."

"No," Miss Pickerell said, smiling. "Rosemary thinks she's too old to play with dolls. I was going to buy it for myself. It reminded me of the past, when life, as you commented, Mr. Lovelace, seemed so much simpler. Mrs. Prism remarked about that, too. 'Those were the days,' she said."

"Mrs. Prism often comes up to the Three Chimney Lodge for lunch," Mr. Lovelace commented.

"But the past was never really simple," Miss Pickerell went on. "We only remember the good parts and think that it was. There were terrible problems then, too. Science has solved many of them."

"Science will solve the problem of oil spills too!" Mortimor Tooting insisted. "You'll see, Miss Pickerell! You'll see!"

"Well," Miss Pickerell said, taking a firm grip on her knitting bag and her umbrella and giving the back of her hair a little pat, "I suppose we'd better go back now. I believe I'll take an evening train home. I really don't like being away from my cat and my cow."

"Wait! Please wait!" Mr. Lovelace begged. "I want to tell you something. I . . . I want to tell you, Miss Pickerell, that I would very much like to be your friend. If . . . if you can ever find it in your heart to forgive me, will you come back to the Three Chimney Lodge?"

Miss Pickerell took her time about answering.

"Maybe," she said, finally, her voice very gentle. "Maybe I'll return. In the spring, when the early flowers will be peeping out of the ground. I'll come with Pumpkins, my cat, and Nancy Agatha, my cow. We'll drive

slowly along the seashore and see the birds
healthy and flying again and the sand white
and clean and the piles of dead sea creatures all gone. I'll bring Mr. Slitherspoon
bottles and bottles of yeast tablets and my
own special recipe for peanut-brittle pie.
And, do you know what else, Mr. Lovelace?
I'll wear a brand new hat, a bright, cheerful hat with both a flower and a ribbon on
it!"

About the Authors

ELLEN MACGREGOR created the character of Miss Pickerell in the early 1950's. With a little help from Miss MacGregor, Lavinia Pickerell had four re-markable adventures. Then, in 1954, Ellen MacGregor died. And it was not until 1964, after a long, long search, that Miss P. finally found Dora Pantell.

DORA PANTELL says that she has been writing some-thing at some time practically since she was born. Among the "somethings" are scripts for radio and television, magazine stories, newspaper articles, books for all ages, and, of course, the Miss Pickerell adventures which, she insists, she enjoys best of all. As good places for writing, she suggests airplanes, dentists' waiting rooms, and a semi-dark theater when the play gets dull. Ms. Pantell spends a good deal of the rest of her time reading non-violent detective stories, listening to classical music on Station WNCN, and watching the television shows on Channel 13, in New York City. But mostly, she is busy keeping the peace among her three cats, Haiku Darling, Eliza Doolittle, and the newest addition, the incorrigible Cluny Brown.

About the Artist

CHARLES GEER has been illustrating for as long as he can remember and has more books to his credit than he can count. He lives in the woods near Flemington, New Jersey, in a log cabin he built himself. When he is not bent over the drawing board or the typewriter—Mr. Geer has written as well as illustrated two middle-group books—he is at work, building a twenty-two foot sailboat, or taking long back-pack hikes, or sailing.